"We are going to get married,"

Slade said. "It's the right thing to do for Andy's sake. And I'm not taking no for an answer. I want the boy to have my name and to know that I wanted to be his father in every sense of the word, including the legal one."

"You don't want me for your wife," Lisa argued. "You made that very clear."

"It's not personal. I don't want any woman for a wife."

"That's supposed to appease me?"

"We were good together. And we both knew how to please each other physically," he said huskily.

Lisa reluctantly admitted to herself that Slade's arguments were valid. Still, she was uneasy. He was asking her to go back to the way they had been before. Well, not exactly. This time she was forewarned. She would know better than to give her heart to him. "All right, I'll marry you…for Andy's sake."

Dear Reader,

The year is off to a wonderful start in Silhouette Romance, and we've got some of our best stories yet for you right here.

Our tremendously successful ROYALLY WED series continues with *The Blacksheep Prince's Bride* by Martha Shields. Our intrepid heroine—a lady-in-waiting for Princess Isabel—will do anything to help rescue the king. Even marry the single dad turned prince! And Judy Christenberry returns to Romance with *Newborn Daddy*. Poor Ryan didn't know what he was missing, until he looked through the nursery window....

Also this month, Teresa Southwick concludes her much-loved series about the Marchetti family in *The Last Marchetti Bachelor*. And popular author Elizabeth August gives us *Slade's Secret Son*. Lisa hadn't planned to tell Slade about their child. But with her life in danger, there's only one man to turn to....

Carla Cassidy's tale of love and adventure is *Lost in His Arms*, while new-to-the-Romance-line Vivienne Wallington proves she's anything but a beginning writer in this powerful story of a man *Claiming His Bride*.

Be sure to come back next month for Valerie Parv's ROYALLY WED title as well as new stories by Sandra Steffen and Myrna Mackenzie. And Patricia Thayer will begin a brand-new series, THE TEXAS BROTHERHOOD.

Happy reading!

Mary-Theresa Hussey

Mary-Theresa Hussey
Senior Editor

Please address questions and book requests to:
Silhouette Reader Service
U.S.: 3010 Walden Ave., P.O. Box 1325, Buffalo, NY 14269
Canadian: P.O. Box 609, Fort Erie, Ont. L2A 5X3

Slade's Secret Son

ELIZABETH AUGUST

SILHOUETTE Romance

Published by Silhouette Books

America's Publisher of Contemporary Romance

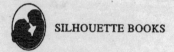

SILHOUETTE BOOKS

ISBN 0-373-19512-5

SLADE'S SECRET SON

Copyright © 2001 by Elizabeth August

This edition published by arrangement with Harlequin Books S.A.

® and TM are trademarks of Harlequin Books S.A., used under license.
Trademarks indicated with ® are registered in the United States Patent
and Trademark Office, the Canadian Trade Marks Office and in other
countries.

Visit Silhouette at www.eHarlequin.com

Printed in U.S.A.

Books by Elizabeth August

ELIZABETH AUGUST

lives in the mountains of North Carolina with her husband, Doug, a chemist. They have three grown sons. Their oldest is pursuing a career in medicine, their middle son is a chemical engineer and their youngest is now in college.

Having survived a bout with cancer, Elizabeth has now joined the ranks of cancer survivors. Writing remains at the top of her list of loves just below her husband, sons and daughter-in-law. Elizabeth has also written under the pseudonym of Betsy Page for Harlequin.

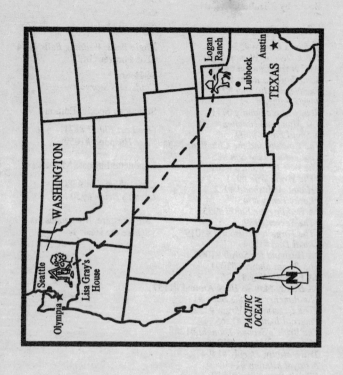

Chapter One

"**W**arts. Warts on top of warts," Lisa Gray cursed under her breath as she parked in front of the modest two-story house on the outskirts of Lubbock, Texas. The white frame structure was set in the midst of twenty-five acres of land. The owner, she knew, liked his privacy and a lot of elbow room. In fact, he was the most determinedly insular person she'd ever known. At one time she'd thought she could change that, but she'd been wrong.

The muscles in her jaw tensed so tightly they threatened to spasm. She hated being here. The urge to turn the rental car around and go back to Seattle was close to overwhelming. Then she shifted her shoulder. A sharp twinge of pain traveled through her, reminding her of why she'd come. "I have to do this. I have no choice." She repeated the liturgy that had gotten her this far.

Climbing out of her car, she made her way to the porch. At the door she hesitated. Then, again telling herself that she had no choice, she rang the bell.

A pleasant-featured, brown-haired, brown-eyed woman opened the door. "Hello."

Silently Lisa berated herself for not checking the phone book to ascertain Slade's current address. It had never occurred to her that he would have moved. This place suited him perfectly. "I'm sorry I bothered you. I thought Slade Logan lived here."

The woman smiled. "He does, but he's not home yet. Would you like to come in and wait?"

Lisa glanced at the woman's left hand. There was a wedding ring. So Slade had remarried. She felt as if a knife was being twisted inside her. Furious that she was letting this affect her so strongly, she ignored the sensation and maintained a facade of indifference. "I'll catch up with him later."

As Lisa started to walk away the woman came outside. "Can I tell him your name?"

Lisa turned back. She'd find another solution. She wasn't certain what, but she'd find one. Again, hurt that he'd remarried cut through her. *I should feel sorry for the woman,* she told herself. Claudette, Slade's first wife who had died tragically, would always be uppermost in his heart. In the next instant Lisa laughed at herself. That was jealousy talking. She'd simply never been able to touch his heart while this woman had.

This admission was the most hurtful yet. Until now she'd blamed Claudette's hold on Slade for him not allowing himself to fall in love with her. Now she had to face the fact that while he'd meant everything to her, she'd been just a warm body to satisfy his needs.

"To be honest, I'm on my way out of town," Lisa said, then she turned and headed back to her car.

"I'm sure he'll be sorry he missed you," the woman called from the porch.

"I doubt that," Lisa muttered under her breath.

The sound of a vehicle approaching caused her to look up the dirt driveway leading to the house. A heavy-duty, four-wheel drive, double-cab, red pickup equipped with an extra roll bar and high-beam spotlights was approaching. It was Slade's truck. Bile rose in her throat as he parked. The last thing she wanted was to witness him with his new wife. But she had no choice. Pride refused to allow her to turn tail and run. Coming to a halt, she stood stiffly.

"Looks like you won't miss him, after all," the woman said, coming off the porch and approaching Lisa.

Lisa barely heard. Her attention was riveted on the tall, muscular Texas Ranger climbing out of the truck. Half Apache, his Native American heritage was obvious in his facial features, his coal-black hair and eyes so dark brown that at times they looked almost ebony. She hated the way the sight of him still caused her heart to pound double time. *You never really meant anything to him,* she snapped at herself, and bitterness for having cared so much for a man who had never honestly cared for her slowed her heart to a more normal rate.

"Lisa," he greeted coolly.

"Slade," she returned with equal coolness.

"Never figured I'd be seeing you again."

The frost in his voice told her that he wished he hadn't. Self-directed anger that she'd come, raged through her. Her gaze shifted to the brown-eyed woman and a flush of embarrassment reddened her cheeks. Not only had she made a fool of herself by coming here, she'd made it in front of Slade's wife. "Sorry I interrupted your evening." Stiffly she added, "Congratulations on your marriage."

The brown-eyed woman grinned, clearly finding this

last statement humorous. "You have the wrong idea."
Extending her hand, she said, "We never introduced our-
selves. I'm Katrina Logan, Slade's sister-in-law. Boyd
and I are just staying here while our place is being
painted."

"Lisa Gray," Lisa responded, accepting the handshake. Even this new knowledge didn't make her feel less
like a fool.

Katrina's gaze shifted between Lisa and Slade. Releasing Lisa's hand, she said, "I think I'll just go inside
and finish cooking dinner. You two look like you've got
some private business to discuss." And, putting action to
her words, she started back toward the house.

Lisa's gaze returned to Slade. The ice was still in his
eyes and nowhere on his face could she find even a hint
of welcome. All the way here she'd waged a constant
battle with her pride and she'd been winning. But his
coldness turned the tide and pride suddenly took control.
"This was a mistake," she said tersely, and turning on
her heels, she strode to her car.

Tears of frustration filled her eyes as she drove away
making Slade a blurred vision in her rearview mirror.
And that was how she wanted him to be...a blurred memory that would eventually fade with time until it was
nothing but a shadow at the back of her mind. But that
wasn't going to happen. She had a reminder of their relationship that would never let Slade be completely
erased from her life the way he had obviously erased her
from his. The tears began to flow down her cheeks.

Slade remained where he was, and frowned at the departing car. Seeing Lisa had been a shock.

She hadn't changed. He remembered the first time he'd
seen her. The rangers had been asked by the Lubbock

police to help with a case and she'd been one of the officers assigned to work with him. The moment she'd entered the room, he'd sensed she was trouble. Five feet, eight inches tall, athletically built, long thick black hair plaited into a single braid that hung down the middle of her back, those jade-green eyes and soft kissable lips... He jerked his mind from the path it was traveling. What had happened between them had ended better than two years ago.

"An old girlfriend?" Katrina asked, returning to Slade's side, her retreat into the house halted by Lisa's abrupt departure.

"Yes."

Surprise registered on Katrina's face and she studied him narrowly. "How old?"

"She left town more than two years ago."

"The family is under the impression you haven't had a serious relationship in the ten years since Claudette died."

"I haven't." The statement tasted like a lie. So maybe Lisa had strolled through his dreams once or twice in the past couple of years. She'd come uninvited. When she'd walked out of his life, he'd been relieved. He didn't want her back.

Katrina frowned thoughtfully. "I wonder why she came."

Silently, Slade admitted to himself that he, too, was surprised Lisa had shown up on his doorstep after all this time. When she'd left, she'd made it clear she had no desire to ever see him again.

His mind flashed back to their final date. They'd gone out to dinner at their favorite restaurant. Lisa had only picked at her food. He'd thought she was preoccupied with a case or was maybe worried about her mother. Her

father had died a couple of years earlier and her mother
had moved to Seattle to live with her mother's sister. The
two older women got along fine most of the time, but
when they had their squabbles her mother would call.
Finally, Lisa had set her fork aside and faced him levelly.
"There is something I need to know," she'd said.

A terse edge in her voice told him that he was the
source of whatever was troubling her. "What?"

"When we first started seeing each other, you made it
clear you never intended to remarry. And, at the time, I
was willing to accept that. But things have changed for
me. I need to know if we have a real future together."
Her jaw had tensed, a sign he'd recognized as an indi-
catio: that this was difficult for her. "I need to know if
there is any possibility that you will reconsider and we
might marry."

"No," he'd answered honestly.

Anger had shown in her eyes. "You would rather continue to live with a ghost than with me?"

"I have my reasons."

"I need more than an affair." She'd risen from the
table. "I do not want to see you again. I'll call a cab to
take me home."

Saying nothing to stop her, he'd simply sat and
watched her walk out. Deep within he'd experienced a
twist of regret, but he'd told himself it was for the best.
She deserved more than he could give.

Less than a month later she'd moved to Seattle to live
with her mother and aunt. They'd kept their affair very
private, even from his own family. Granted Boyd had
known Slade had dated her, but even he'd been made to
understand that their relationship was not an emotional
one. So there had been no gossip at work nor any out-
siders trying to get them back together. During the short

time she'd remained in Lubbock, she'd avoided him as much as possible and, he admitted, he'd avoided her. There had been only one final encounter. He shoved that memory from his mind.

"I got the impression she didn't really want to be here," Katrina mused out loud, jerking Slade's mind back to the present. "Must have been something important. She certainly wasn't here for a social call."

Slade had to admit that Katrina was right. So, why had Lisa come here?

A blue pickup similar to Slade's came down the driveway, parked beside Slade's vehicle, and a man also wearing the badge of a Texas Ranger climbed out of the cab. "I swear I just passed Lisa Gray on the road," Boyd Logan, a younger version of Slade, said, striding toward his wife and brother.

"You did," Katrina replied.

"You chased her off again?" Boyd frowned at Slade. "I only met her a couple of times, but I was under the impression she was not only a terrific police officer, she was a good woman...strong, honest."

"I didn't chase her off the first time," Slade replied. "She just figured there was nothing worth staying for."

Boyd shook his head at his brother. "If you don't learn to put the past behind you, you're never going to have a future."

Slade's jaw hardened. "I'm satisfied with my life just the way it is."

Boyd didn't look convinced, but let the subject drop. "So why was Lisa here?"

"She didn't say," Slade replied.

Boyd raised an eyebrow. "She came all the way from Seattle and didn't say why?"

A part of Slade wanted to let Lisa go her own way,

but a stronger part couldn't. Katrina was right. Lisa wouldn't have come here without a very strong reason. "Think I'd better find out why she came."

Boyd nodded his agreement.

"Looks like you won't have to go far." Katrina motioned toward the road with twist of her head.

The men turned to see Lisa's car returning.

"Boyd and I'll just go in the kitchen and finish cooking dinner," Katrina said, taking hold of her husband's arm and pulling him along with her.

Slade didn't even acknowledge their departure. He was already on his way to meet Lisa as she climbed out of her car. "What's going on?" He read the proud defiance on her face. "Must be something real important to make you overcome that pride of yours."

Lisa swallowed the lump of rebellion that had formed in her throat. "It is." She steeled herself and met his gaze. "There's something I need to tell you."

Slade could see how much this was costing her. "Then tell me."

"I want you to know that I would never have come here if I'd had any other option."

"That's pretty obvious," Slade said, noting that the strain lines in her face were deepening by the second.

Her jaw tensed even more. "I took a bullet three weeks ago. I was lucky. A quarter of an inch to the right and I would have been dead. My mortality is why I'm here. I'd never really come to grips with it before."

The thought of her close brush with death caused a spasm of fear for her to race through him. "I'm glad you're all right."

Lisa read the honesty in his eyes. There was even a touch of warmth. *That's not going to last long.* "Anyway, I realized that if I'd died..." She paused to swallow the lump that had again formed in her throat. "I never wanted to ask you for anything, but my mother is too old and not in a financial position to take on the responsibility of raising a child."

Slade's gaze narrowed on her. "Child?"

Lisa breathed a terse sigh. "Our son."

He had a son. A surge of joy, pride and excitement he'd never expected to ever experience mingled within him. These emotions were followed by anger. "You had my child and weren't even going to tell me?"

"You refused to open your heart to me. You've made it into a shrine to Claudette. I figured you wouldn't want a child of mine. And I'm not asking you for anything for either of us right now. We're doing just fine on our own. As long as nothing happens to me, you'll never have to concern yourself about us. I just want your word that if anything does happen to me, you'll see that Andy is taken care of."

"You're joking, right? You think I'll just walk away from my child?"

Lisa was tempted to point out that he'd had no trouble walking away from her, but bit back the words. She didn't want him to know how much he'd hurt her. "I didn't come here to invite you into our lives. I came here because I want to know my son has a safety net."

"*Our* son. And I intend to be a great deal more than a safety net to him."

Lisa had convinced herself that while Slade would do his duty by Andy and see that the boy was looked after if anything happened to her, he would be perfectly happy to stay on the sidelines unless involving himself in Andy's life became necessary. She had, in fact, been certain he would be grateful to her for not telling him she'd gotten pregnant and for allowing him to remain on his own. Apparently she'd been wrong on this point.

"Where is he? I want to see him."

"He's in Seattle with my mother."

Slade caught her by the arm and began pulling her along with him toward the house. "I'm calling my commander and telling him that I need a few days off. Then we're booking the first flight to Seattle."

A spasm of pain from her healing wound shot through Lisa, but it was the way her body reacted to his touch that shook her to the core. After all this time he could still make her blood race. "Let go of me."

Slade heard the edge of pain in her voice. Coming to an abrupt halt, he released her. "I'm sorry. I forgot you'd been shot," he apologized gruffly. "This has been a shock." His jaw hardened. "I know I'm partially to blame for you not coming to me when you discovered you were pregnant, but the boy's my blood and I will do right by him and you."

"I suppose you should at least meet him," Lisa conceded.

Slade motioned for her to precede him into the house and Lisa obeyed. Like a physical contact, she could feel his eyes on her back. A warm tingling started at the nape of her neck and began to work its way through her. Silently she cursed. She wanted to be as immune to him as he was to her.

In the living room, the exhaustion from her trip mingled with her anxiety over facing Slade caught up with her and she sank down onto the couch while Slade punched numbers into the phone. Watching him, she was certain that once he got over the shock of being a father, his determined allegiance to Claudette would cause him to lose interest in a child that wasn't hers.

"We heard you come in…" Katrina's cheerful greeting died in her throat as she and Boyd entered the living room and she saw Lisa. Concern spread over her features. "Are you all right? You look pale."

"I'm still recovering from a bullet wound," Lisa replied, not wanting them to guess that Slade's presence had anything to do with how shaken she was feeling.

Boyd took a stride closer. "You suffer any serious damage?"

"No." She'd always liked Boyd. He was a kind man, strong and dependable…like Slade in a lot of ways, but without the dark brooding side created by Slade's haunting past.

Boyd smiled with relief. "Glad to hear that."

"You look like you could use something to eat. I've got a pot roast ready to be served. There's plenty. Come join us," Katrina coaxed.

Lisa considered refusing. But her stomach growled, reminding her that she hadn't eaten all day. Reasoning that some of the effect Slade was having on her could be due to light-headedness caused by lack of food, she nodded gratefully. "Thanks. I'll take you up on that invitation."

Boyd had been catching bits of Slade's conversation. As his brother hung up, he turned to him. "Heard you tell the commander you were going to take some time off. What's going on?"

Slade's gaze came to rest on Lisa. "It seems I have a son I'd never have learned about if Lisa hadn't had her brush with death." His jaw hardened into a grim line. "I would have married you."

Ignoring the surprised looks on Boyd's and Katrina's faces, Lisa met his gaze with defiance. "I wanted a man who loved me, not one who prefers to live with a ghost and would only marry me because I was pregnant with his child and he felt it was the only honorable thing to do.''

For a long moment Slade regarded her in stoic silence. Then, heading to the doorway, he said curtly, "I've got reservations to make and a bag to pack.''

Chapter Two

Seated on the plane a few hours later, Slade recalled how Boyd and Katrina had reacted to his news. They'd been shocked, but he'd seen the understanding in their eyes when Lisa had said she didn't want a man who preferred to live with a ghost. His jaw tensed. He had his reasons.

Returning his thoughts to his brother and sister-in-law, he pictured them and Lisa at the dinner table. Lisa had been obviously uneasy, but Katrina and Boyd had done their best to make her feel less awkward. They'd even expressed excitement at having a nephew. His expression hardened. And the rest of his family had better behave as well or they'd be answering to him.

Pushing his family to the back of his mind, Slade studied Lisa covertly as the plane taxied down the runway, then rose into the sky. She was more pale than normal and he recalled how she'd winced when he'd pulled on her arm. "How did you get shot?"

She'd begun to wonder if he was even going to ask or

if his feelings toward her were so shallow, he really
didn't care. "I was in the wrong place at the wrong time.
When I moved to Seattle, I decided to not join the police
force. I wanted more flexible working hours so I started
my own detective agency and hooked up with a couple
of groups of lawyers, doing investigations, serving subpoenas...the legwork kind of stuff.

"Anyway, I was serving divorce papers on a guy
named Tommy Cross. He was a medium-class hood
who'd been caught in a sting operation. People were dis-
tancing themselves fast and furiously from him. Even
though the man's Mr. Stonewall himself, someone must
have been worried that he might cut a deal and name
names. They took a shot at him, missed and hit me instead."

Abruptly she grinned dryly. "Talk about a 'shot heard
'round Seattle and further.' Tommy didn't take well to
being a target. But I think what bugged him the most was
that he'd given his word that he'd be silent and he hadn't
been believed. Tommy always prided himself on keeping
his word. The next thing the locals knew, he was talking
his head off. He knew so much, it crossed state lines and
they had to bring in the Feds."

Slade recognized the glitter of excitement in her eyes.
She liked action, especially when it went well. He recalled the way his stomach had knotted when he'd heard
about some of her exploits in the field. She believed in
getting her man, even if it involved personal injury. Anger that she took placing her life in jeopardy so lightly
built inside of him. "You have a child. And until today,
you were raising him on your own. I can't believe you
are still being so cavalier about risking your life."

Lisa glared at him. "I was never cavalier about my

life. I was doing my job, the same as you and every other lawman.''

Maybe he was being unfairly critical, Slade admitted to himself. Law enforcement was innately a dangerous occupation. Still... "The problem is that if there's trouble anywhere in your vicinity, you seem to find it.''

"I do not." When they'd been dating, he'd said that he accepted her being in danger as part of her job, but there had been a couple of times when he'd come close to overreacting when she'd had a close call. At those times, a shuttered look had descended over his features and she'd wondered if maybe he did care for her more than he'd wanted to admit. *Stupid girl.* It was fantasies like that that had caused her to think he might fall in love with her. But he hadn't. He would never betray his precious Claudette.

Slade told himself to drop the subject, but he couldn't. That she'd had such a close brush with death continued to taunt him. "I'd have thought that with a child depending on you, you'd have found a less dangerous occupation."

"And I thought I had found a safer venue," she snapped back, angered by the accusatory tone in his voice. "The jobs I took were mostly paperwork type of investigating...going through state, federal and county records, checking out phone bills, bank records, that kind of stuff. There was some surveillance, but nothing anyone would consider dangerous." Her jaw tensed defensively. "I didn't want to burden you with a child you didn't want so I ignored the fact that no one's life is guaranteed."

"I thought you knew me better than that. I would always want to be involved in the life of any child I fathered," Slade returned curtly.

To herself, she admitted that she had known that. It

had been her pride that had kept her from telling him until now. That, and one other worry. "There is one thing I won't abide. I won't allow you to make my son feel second best to the child Claudette was carrying when she died. Even if you think that, you'd better keep it hidden from him or you'll have me to answer to."

As angry as he was for having been kept in the dark about his son, Slade knew he had to accept some of the blame. He had been adamant about never loving anyone except for Claudette. It was only reasonable for Lisa to assume he might feel the same about his and Claudette's unborn child. But she was wrong. Any child he fathered would be special to him. With every passing moment his need to see his son, to hold him, was growing in intensity. "I promise you, he will never be made to feel second best. I was raised to believe that every child is uniquely special."

He sounded sincere, but although she would have accepted his word on anything else, her son was too important to her. She'd keep a close eye on Slade. At the first sign that he was comparing Andy to the child he'd envisioned having with Claudette, she'd boot Slade out of their lives. Giving in to exhaustion, she closed her eyes and slept.

Between delayed flights and scheduled layovers, dawn was nearly breaking when they finally landed in Seattle. Driving to the house she and Andy shared with her mother and aunt, Lisa grew more and more tense. Slade had never been one to make small talk and the silence in the car felt deafening.

"What have you told Andy about me?" He asked, abruptly breaking the stillness.

"Nothing. He's barely two years old and, so far, he

hasn't asked about his father so I've never said anything."

Slade studied her narrowly. "What were you going to tell him when he did finally ask?"

"To be honest, I wasn't really sure." Her shoulders stiffened defensively. "But I wouldn't have told him anything that would have turned him against you."

"Just the fact that I wasn't contributing to his upbringing in any way would have done that."

"I did what I thought was the right thing to do at the time."

Slade held back an angry retort. In all fairness, he knew he couldn't entirely fault her. He'd so much as told her that he didn't want a relationship that went beyond the surface.

No further conversation passed between them until they were pulling into the driveway of the huge old two-story home in one of the older districts of Seattle. Again, it was Slade who broke the silence. "I like to know what I'm walking into. Just how opposed are your aunt and mother to my being here."

"They're uneasy, but not really opposed. They're afraid you don't honestly want Andy and that he'll sense it and feel rejected."

"I would never do that to him."

Lisa knew he believed what he was saying and, as a mother, she felt her son was so adorable that anyone would fall in love with him. However, having been stung by Slade's past herself, she vowed to not allow her son to be equally harmed.

Entering the house, they smelled coffee brewing along with the aroma of freshly baked cinnamon rolls. Before they could close the door behind them, two women came out of the kitchen. The one in the lead, Slade judged to be in her fifties. With her green eyes and once black hair, now streaked with gray, she was an older version of Lisa. The woman following her, whom he guessed to be in her sixties, also bore a strong family resemblance.

"We both woke early and couldn't go back to sleep," the younger of the two women said, her voice curt with anxiety as she studied Lisa, then turned her gaze to Slade.

Lisa forced a calmness she wasn't feeling into her manner. "Mother, this is Slade. Slade this is my mother, Helen Gray."

Slade extended his hand. "Pleased to meet you."

Helen accepted the handshake but made no response.

"And this is my aunt, Ester Kelso." Lisa completed the introductions.

"Pleased to meet you," Slade said, extending his hand to her, as well.

"I'm not ready to say the same about you," Ester replied, accepting the handshake but continuing to regard him with distrust.

"Aunt Ester," Lisa admonished sternly.

"Ester can be a bit too outspoken," Helen said. "But she is merely saying out loud what I'm thinking, as well." A fierce protectiveness glistened in her eyes as she, too, turned her full attention on Slade. "We won't stand by and allow you to harm Andy in any way."

Slade glowered at the women. "I've come here to accept my responsibility as his father. If I had known about the pregnancy, I would have married Lisa and taken care of her and our child from the beginning." He turned to Lisa, his jaw set in a resolute line. "It's never too late to right a wrong. I've given this situation some thought and decided that we have to get married. And it should be done as quickly as possible."

Lisa had always known Slade was a man who lived

by a strong code of duty. She also knew that it was duty and nothing more that was the reason he was willing to marry her. Her shoulders straightened with pride. "I didn't bring you into Andy's and my life because I wanted you for a husband."

"And I will not allow my son to go through life as a bastard. We will marry and I will have his name changed to Logan. I want him to know that he is as much a member of my family as he is of yours."

"We can have his name changed without you and me marrying."

"That's not enough. I want him to be able to say his parents were married. I know that sounds old-fashioned, but that's the way I am."

Helen stepped between her daughter and Slade. "I realize that life might be a lot easier for Andy if he has a father who wants to claim him, but I will not allow you to bully Lisa into doing something she thinks is wrong."

Ester placed herself beside her sister, forming a human wall between Lisa and Slade. "And neither will I."

They reminded Slade of the women in his own family…strong-willed, determined, self-reliant and stubborn. "I'm just trying to do right by my child."

Even though Lisa was still not certain Slade would be able to find a real place in his heart for her son, she found herself coming to his defense. He was, she knew for certain, a man of honor. "I know Slade means well," she said, stepping out from behind the protective barrier.

Aware of her doubts about him as a father, Slade was surprised by the conviction in her voice.

"I suppose we really didn't have any other option but to bring him in on this," Helen said with a heavy sigh, still not looking convinced that this had been the best course of action.

Ester continued to stare sternly at Slade. "Our Lisa is a wonderful woman. No man in his right mind would ever consider her second best. She's strictly first-rate."

So, Lisa had been honest with them about why she'd kept their child a secret. "I've always respected Lisa. I know she's a first-rate person."

Both Helen and Ester tossed him disgruntled glances, letting him know they found his response less than satisfactory.

"She's a woman any man should be proud to *love*," Helen snapped, and Ester nodded curtly.

"It's been a long trip," Lisa interrupted. She'd confessed to her aunt and mother that she'd been in love with Slade and hoped that he'd fall in love with her. Even if Slade had guessed that was the case, she didn't want them confirming it by blurting it out. "I'll show Slade to his room."

"There's coffee and fresh cinnamon rolls in the kitchen," Ester said.

"As soon as we've freshened up, we'll be down," Lisa returned, motioning Slade toward the stairs.

Picking up both his and her satchel, Slade nodded his goodbye to her mother and aunt, then waited for Lisa to precede him up the stairs. When they reached the second-floor landing, he stepped in front of her, stopping her. "I want to see my son."

Lisa, too, was anxious to see her child. The mere sight of him gave her strength. "He's asleep and I don't want to wake him," she cautioned as they neared a room, the entrance blocked by a child's safety gate.

From the doorway, Slade peered inside. The window shade was up, allowing early morning light to give dim illumination to the interior. His gaze went immediately to the twin-size bed nestled in the corner. The top and one side each against a wall, a child's bed rail protected the side open to the room. Realizing Lisa was not about to open the gate that separated him from his son, Slade frowned. "I want a closer look."

"I told you, I don't want to wake him."

"Mommy?" A small voice issued from the bed.

In the next instant there was movement as the occupant of the bed wiggled to the open bottom end, climbed off and headed for the door. He was rubbing his eyes, a sign he was still in the process of waking. Halfway across the room, he looked in the direction of his destination. Abruptly, he came to a halt.

Lisa wasn't surprised. Slade was an imposing figure. But she didn't want her son's first encounter with his father to leave any taste of fear. Quickly she switched on the light. "Hi, sweetheart," she said, smiling warmly as she unfastened the gate.

Andy stood rooted, staring at the tall, dark stranger in the doorway.

"It's all right," Lisa soothed, then realized that there was no fear on Andy's face. Instead, he was studying Slade with a guarded speculation, his expression a child's version of the one she'd seen on Slade's face so many times when he encountered someone for the first time and wasn't certain if they were friend or foe.

Glancing over her shoulder, Lisa saw that Slade had not moved. He was standing like a statue in the doorway, staring down at their child. The thought that he was disappointed at the sight of his son caused a rush of rage inside her. Motherly pride bubbled to the surface. Suddenly a look of tenderness, so intense it took her breath away, spread over Slade's features.

It took all of Slade's willpower to not stride into the room and pick up his son. He didn't want to frighten the boy. There was no doubt that this was his child. Andy was the exact image of him at that age. But then, he'd never for a moment questioned Lisa's honesty. Remaining in the doorway, he squatted so that he was at eye level with his child, then said in an easy drawl, "I'm real pleased to be meeting you."

Andy remained where he was, his head cocked to one side, and continued to study the man.

Lisa held out her hand to her son. "I want you to meet Slade Logan," she coaxed.

Andy accepted her hand and walked with her toward Slade, stopping a couple of feet in front of him.

"Slade's a friend." Lisa saw Slade's jaw twitch with controlled anger and added, "He's also your father."

"Sllaade," Andy said, as if tasting the feel of the name on his tongue.

"You can call me dad." Slade wanted to waste no time establishing his true position.

Watching the two of them, Lisa found herself thinking how much alike they were. She'd known Andy resembled his father but until now she'd never realized just how much. And the resemblance wasn't merely physical, either. Andy's mannerisms, the way he held himself, the way he faced his father right now, studying him with guarded interest...all of these things combined into a miniature Slade.

Lisa could tell by looking at him that with every fiber of his being, Slade wanted to pick up his son and hug him. Instead he extended his hand and said, "How about a handshake?"

Releasing his hold on his mother's hand, Andy took another step toward the man and placed his hand in Slade's.

Slade's huge hand swallowed up the toddler's. The desire to hold on to the boy forever was strong, but Slade made himself release his hold after only a moment.

"Sllaade," Andy repeated with a smile that indicated he'd decided to accept the man as a friend.

"Dad," Slade corrected with a crooked grin to let the boy know that he, too, considered them friends.

Andy looked up at his mother as if confused by this double name.

"Dad. You should call him dad," Lisa responded to the question in her son's eyes. Silently she prayed that, for her son's sake, the tenderness she'd seen on Slade's face would remain untainted by the ghosts that haunted him.

Andy turned back to Slade. "Daa," he said as if imprinting the name in his memory bank.

A lump the size of Texas formed in Slade's throat. "Son," he said around it, and ruffled Andy's hair. "Think I could have a hug?" he coaxed.

Lisa was stunned by the depth of feeling she read on Slade's face. She'd never seen this openly loving side of him. He'd been tender with her, kind, generous and thoughtful, but she'd always been aware of the wall he kept between himself and her. For a moment jealousy that her son had been allowed to enter Slade's heart while she'd always be left on the outside flowed through her. Then pride came to her rescue. She refused to waste emotions on a man who preferred a ghost to a real flesh-and-blood woman. "Give your father a hug," she encouraged, giving Andy a small nudge toward Slade.

Andy hesitated for a second, then with a crooked grin that matched Slade's, he opened his arms, approached Slade and wrapped them around Slade's neck.

Emotions too strong to even categorize pervaded Slade as he wound his arms around his son. Feeling Andy attempting to wiggle free, Slade forced himself to release the boy.

Satisfied he'd been properly introduced to the stranger and the stranger was not a threat, Andy turned to his mother and held up his arms to her.

''I suppose you want to get dressed and have some breakfast.'' Because her shoulder was still too sore to allow her to pick him up, she knelt, wrapped her arms around him and nuzzled his neck.

Andy nodded vigorously.

Feeling the need to have some time alone with her son, Lisa rose and, holding her son by the hand, headed to the door. ''We'll just show your father to his room first.''

Slade knew she was trying to get rid of him and wanted to protest, but stopped himself. His relationship with his son was still on shaky ground and he didn't want to do anything that would evoke anger from Lisa in front of the boy. Picking up both her satchel and his, he said, ''I'll drop your satchel off at your room.''

Relieved he wasn't going to give her any argument, Lisa nodded toward the next door on the same side of the hall as Andy's room. ''That's my room,'' she said.

Slade dropped her bag just inside, while she paused in the hall.

She nodded toward a door on the other side of the passage. ''That'll be your room.''

Pleased that he would be so close to his son's room, Slade smiled. ''Thanks.'' With a final wink toward Andy, he entered his room.

Lisa had finished changing Andy's diaper and was dressing him when she felt a prickling along her spine. Without turning around, she was certain it was Slade in the doorway watching her. From the first time they'd met, she'd been acutely aware of his presence. She'd hoped that had faded during the past couple of years. Obviously, it hadn't.

Andy peered around her. "Da," he said, confirming what she already knew.

Approaching them, Slade held his arms out toward the boy. "Can I give you a lift downstairs?"

Lisa expected Andy to refuse. He was cautious around strangers. Even more, Slade had an intimidating effect on people. The first time they'd met, he'd gone immediately to the top of her list of men she most wanted to avoid in the future. *I would have been smart to have followed that instinct,* she admonished herself. Then she thought of Andy and retracted that thought. Her son was precious to her and she would never regret having him.

Andy cocked his head and again studied the tall, mountain of a man while his mother finished tying his shoe. When she was done, he slid off of his bed and stood beside her for a long moment, then clearly making up his mind, he held out his arms toward Slade.

Grinning with pleasure, Slade picked up his son.

They were a matched pair, Lisa thought, watching the two of them together. Her pride still stung some, but she was forced to admit that bringing Slade and his son together had been the right thing to do.

Chapter Three

Lisa woke groggily. Both she and Slade had caught short naps in the airports and on the flights to Seattle, but she was still recovering from her wound and by the time Andy was settled in to eat his breakfast, exhaustion had forced her to go to her room to lie down. She'd immediately fallen asleep. Now she was being gently shaken awake.

Opening her eyes, she saw Slade. Fear that something had happened to Andy raced through her. "What's wrong?" she asked, bolting into an upright position. Before she could get to her feet, dizziness forced her to stop and hold her head in her hands.

Slade's hands closed around her shoulders, adding support. "Are you all right?"

"Head rush," she replied, furious that her body wasn't healing as quickly as she wanted it to. Even more disconcerting was the soothing heat his touch was spreading through her. She didn't want him affecting her that way. She wanted to feel neutral toward him. Giving her shoulders a small twist to indicate she wanted him to release her, she sucked in a groan of discomfort.

"I was just trying to help," Slade said impatiently, releasing her and taking a step back.

Lisa berated herself for overreacting, but then she'd never been able to keep herself entirely under control where Slade was concerned. The nausea now subsiding, her original panic returned. "Has something happened to Andy?"

"Andy's fine," Slade assured her. Tenderness again softened his feature. "He and I have been getting acquainted. Smart little guy and full of energy."

Lisa saw the love in Slade's eyes. Clearly, he'd allowed Andy into his heart and, for her son's sake, she was glad.

"It's getting late and I want to go get our marriage license today."

Glancing at the clock on the bedside table, Lisa saw that it was after two. "I slept half the day?"

"You needed the rest. You're still recovering from your wound."

"Where's Andy?"

"He's taking his nap." Slade backed up further so that he could lean against the wall. "He's very devoted to you. A couple of times every hour he insisted on coming in and checking on you."

Her son's concern caused a motherly warmth to spread through her and she was forced to admit that deep inside she'd been worried that Slade had such a powerful presence, Andy might become so enamored of him, he would forget about her when Slade was present. "He is a very caring child," she said with pride.

"You've done well by him." Slade straightened with purpose. "And now it's my turn to do right by him.

While he's napping, we're going to go get our marriage license. Your mother is making you a sandwich you can eat on the way.''

Lisa's jaw firmed. "I am not going to marry you. That is not why I brought you into this."

"We are going to get married. It's the right thing to do for Andy's sake. And I'm not taking no for an answer. I want the boy to have my name and to know that I wanted to be his father in every sense of the word, including the legal one.''

Lisa scowled. "You don't want me for your wife. You made that very clear.''

"It's not personal. I don't want any woman for a wife.''

"That's supposed to appease me?''

"If you don't let me marry you, Andy might always think that I didn't really want him. I don't want him to have any doubts about the bond I feel toward him.''

"I'll explain that it was my choice.''

"And then there's the legal system," Slade persisted. "If anything happens to you, the courts might look at it differently. You and I both know that you can't count on a judge to always do the right thing. If we never marry, a court could rule against my getting custody. And, if the court feels that your mother and aunt can't care for him properly, Andy could even end up in the foster care system.''

Lisa had to concede that there was a small chance things could turn out as he predicted, a very small chance but a possibility nonetheless, and that thought sent a chill of fear through her.

"We were good together," Slade continued. "We have the same tastes, a lot of the same interests, and we both know how to please each other physically. I'd say we probably have more going for us than a lot of couples who marry."

Lisa reluctantly admitted to herself that his arguments were valid. Still, she was uneasy. He was asking her to go back to the way they had been before. Well, not exactly. This time she was forewarned. She would know better than to give her heart to him. "All right, I'll marry you for Andy's sake. But if the marriage doesn't work out, I want your word that you'll give me a divorce and not fight me for custody."

"I'll want joint custody."

"I don't want him bounced back and forth between us. I want primary custody and I get to set the conditions."

Slade recognized the determined look on her face. If he wanted her to marry him, he was going to have to make concessions. "I want your word that you'll be fair."

It hurt that he didn't trust her, but then, she hadn't exactly demonstrated an unquestionable trust in him, either. "You have my word."

"And you have my word."

"Then give me a few minutes to pull myself together." She looked down at the outfit she'd been wearing for two days now and wrinkled her nose. "I need to shower and put on fresh clothes."

Following Slade's exit, Lisa stood for a long moment frowning at the closed door. She told herself that she should be pleased he was being so "civilized" about this matter. But then that's what she should have expected. Slade Logan was a man in total control of himself... A practical man who had a firm conviction of what was right and what was wrong, of what his duty was, and he had the ability to act on those principles without allowing his emotions to interfere with reason.

Lisa had finished showering and just returned to her room to dress when a knock sounded on her door, immediately followed by the entry of her aunt and her mother.

"Ester and I have been discussing your situation and we're not sure marrying Slade Logan is the right thing to do," Helen blurted, the moment the door was closed.

"We've done fine on our own," Ester added.

"I'm doing this to assure Andy's future in case something happens to me," Lisa explained. She looked to her mother. "You're fifty-three. You'll be seventy-three before Andy is even twenty-one." She didn't even point out that Ester would be into her eighties.

"We just aren't certain you should be tying yourself to a man for the sake of a child," Helen said worriedly.

"I'm not *tying* myself to him. I have his word that if the marriage doesn't suit me, we'll get a divorce and I'll have primary custody of Andy without a fight."

"Do you have that in writing?" Ester demanded.

"I have Slade's word."

"I think you should get it in writing," Helen encouraged.

Lisa understood their concern and if she'd been dealing with any man other than Slade Logan she would have insisted on having the agreement in writing, as well, but in that moment she realized how fully she trusted him. "Like I said before, Slade is a man of honor. If I doubted that, I would never have gone to him. His word is his bond."

Ester pursed her lips into a displeased pout and Lisa braced herself. That look meant her aunt was preparing an all-out assault to get what she wanted. Glancing at her mother, she saw the same expression on Helen's face.

Then, abruptly, Ester shrugged, the pout disappeared and was replaced by her "I have the solution" look. Heading out the door, she said over her shoulder, "If that's true, he won't mind putting it in writing."

Nodding her head in agreement, Helen followed her sister.

"Leave Slade alone," Lisa called after them, but even as she issued the order, she knew it was falling on deaf ears. Quickly dressing, she raced downstairs. She found Slade in the kitchen with her mother and aunt. He was sitting at the table writing out something on a piece of paper. "This isn't necessary," Lisa said, her cheeks flushing with embarrassment.

"If it puts your mother's and your aunt's minds at ease then it is," Slade returned, continuing to write as he spoke.

Lisa gave the two older women an angry, impatient look. "I really can't believe you did this."

Ester regarded her with self-righteous dignity. "I watch those court shows on television all the time and this is just the sort of thing the judge advises all the defendants to do."

"Slade and I are nothing like the people you see on those shows," Lisa snapped, her embarrassment building.

"I'll bet that's what some of those people thought before they ended up there," Ester returned.

Lisa gave her aunt a "you're impossible" glance, then turned her attention to Slade. "I am truly sorry about this. I told them that you were a man of your word." Again she gave her mother and aunt an angry glare. "In fact, I've told them that several times."

Slade scrawled his signature at the bottom of the paper,

then looked up at her. "The fact that you didn't come to me when you found out you were pregnant probably has a lot to do with their distrust. I've written out this paper to prove to them that I would never intentionally cause you or our son any grief or harm."

Behind his polite demeanor, she caught the edge of reprimand in his voice and bristled. "I did what I thought was right. I've never claimed to be perfect." Her gaze turned on her mother and aunt. "And now I realize that was a mistake, so I'm correcting it." Her gaze shifted back to Slade. "And I don't need you chiding me for my original decision. It was based solely on your attitude toward marriage." Her attention went back to her mother and aunt. "And my current decision is based on concern for my son. I'm doing what I believe has to be done to insure Andy's future."

All three of them regarded her indulgently, then, picking up the paper Slade had just signed, Helen said, "I'll put this in a safe place," and left the room with Ester following close behind.

Slade rose from the table. "Are you ready?"

Lisa nodded stiffly.

"You don't have to look as if you're going to the dentist to have a root canal," he muttered as they left the house and walked to her car.

Lisa made no response but a little voice warned that a root canal would be like a walk in the park compared to the pain she would experience if she ever allowed the feelings she'd had for Slade to again breathe life.

A while later Lisa was as taut as a bowstring as she and Slade walked back to her car. Getting the marriage license had been incredibly easy...no blood tests, no identification. And they'd left with the document in hand.

In three days it would be valid and they could be married by any priest, rabbi or recognized minister of any denomination, or by any state judge.

All during the process, Lisa had observed Slade. He'd been stiff, almost cardboardlike, making it clear to her that while he may be willing to go through the motions, for him this marriage was simply a legal means to achieve his ends. She was certain that as soon as Andy's name had been changed and Slade's position as Andy's father affirmed, he'd want out of their marriage. Pride bubbled within her. "After we go through the ceremony, just because we have a piece of paper that says we're married doesn't mean I'm going to jump back into your bed."

Slade gave her an impatient look. "Once we go through that ceremony, we will be married and I intend for that marriage to be a long and lasting one."

Lisa's jaw firmed with resolve. "I'm not sharing a bed with a ghost. I did it once. I'm not doing it again."

Slade caught her by the arm and brought her to a halt. "We've got a son to raise. He needs both a mother and a father, preferably under the same roof. I want your promise that you'll at least give our marriage a chance."

His touch was like a match igniting a fire deep within her. Rage that she was still so attracted to him spread through her. "Before I make any promises, I want your promise that you'll try to finally bury Claudette and let me into your heart." When Slade made no response, she glared at him. "I hope you and your ghost have a happy life, but don't plan on me sharing it."

His jaw twitched, then as if the words were being ripped from him, he said, "I can't go through that kind of loss again. Once was enough."

So that was it! He clung to Claudette because he was

afraid to love again. Lisa studied the resolute line of his jaw. She would never be able to break through the barrier he'd created around his heart. She'd tried once and ended up getting hurt. There was no doubt in her mind the same thing would happen again. "Once was enough for me, too," she muttered under her breath. Jerking free from his hold, she headed across the street. Hearing a car's engine start up, she glanced to her left and saw a black sedan pull out of a parking space. She picked up her pace to get out of its lane.

Slade hung back, deciding to let the car pass before he crossed. He couldn't blame Lisa for wanting more than he was willing to give, but he wasn't ready to abandon the idea of them making a life together. He enjoyed her company and he wanted to be an everyday part of his son's life.

A sudden prickling, the kind he always experienced when something wasn't right, jerked his attention to the oncoming vehicle. It was speeding up and heading directly toward Lisa. Reaching her on the run, he caught her by the waist and carried her with him through the space between her car and the one behind it. The sound of metal impacting metal filled the air as they tumbled to the ground unbalanced by Slade's rescue.

"Ouch." Lisa groaned when her body impacted with the hard earth, sending a jolt of pain through her.

"Sorry," Slade apologized, quickly getting to his feet in time to see the sedan speeding away.

Lisa shifted into a sitting position. "What was that all about?"

Slade moved to where he could get a look at the damage done to the side of her car. "Someone just tried to run you down."

She stared at him in disbelief. "Run *me* down?"

"Sure looked that way." He headed back to her. "Stay down."

Lisa's first instinct was to disobey, to prove to him that she could take care of herself. Then she thought of Andy and remained where she was.

"I assume you have a gun. Is it in your purse?"

"I didn't bring it with me."

Slade's gaze hardened. "It looks like that sniper might not have missed his target, after all."

"I can't believe this," Lisa muttered. "Who would want to kill me?"

A man came running out of the building they'd exited. "I saw the whole thing. Looked like that guy was trying to hit you."

A couple of other people were also rushing toward them from other directions.

"I'm not sitting here on the ground with a crowd gathering around," Lisa said, beginning to work herself to her feet.

Agreeing that her staying down would serve no purpose now and remaining immobile could even place her in danger, Slade gave her a hand, keeping her close and shielding her as much as possible with his body.

Reaching them, the man studied Lisa worriedly. "You look pretty shaken. Couldn't believe the way the guy barreled down on you." Abruptly he grinned. "I got part of the license plate."

Keeping Lisa between himself and the car, Slade opened the passenger side door. "Get in and duck down," he ordered. "Could be your sniper wasn't the driver and he's hidden somewhere to finish the job in case the driver missed."

Lisa obeyed. She was scared and hurting and glad

Slade was there. He was bull-headed and too authoritative at times, but right now he made her feel safe.

"She hurt?" the man asked.

"She's pretty shaken."

"I called the police and an ambulance," a woman said, joining them, a cell phone in her hand.

More people began to gather.

"Did any of you see the driver?" Slade asked.

"I think it was a man," a slender man offered.

"Who could tell?" The pale-blond woman beside him gave him a wry look. "Whoever it was was wearing a hat pulled way down and sunglasses."

"It was just an impression." The slender man defended himself.

Further arguing between the two was cut short by the sound of approaching police and ambulance sirens.

Slade was getting more and more uneasy by the moment as the crowd grew. "Stay back," he ordered those approaching. "This is a crime scene."

"Yeah, he's right." The man who'd gotten part of the license plate spread his arms, forming a barrier, and eased people back.

Opening the car door, Slade looked in at Lisa crouched low in the seat. "How do you feel? Do you need the paramedics to take a look at you?"

"No. I'm just shaken, but I'm fine," she assured him.

"Good. The less exposure, the better." Closing the door, he continued to rake the crowd with his gaze, looking for anyone who might pose a threat to Lisa.

"What happened here?" one of the two patrolmen who had just arrived demanded, approaching Slade.

"Someone tired to run my fiancée down," he replied. His attention shifted to the paramedics who were coming on the run. "She doesn't need medical attention." Returning his gaze to the policeman, he added, "I think it would be best if I get her someplace sheltered."

The second of the two patrolmen eyed Slade skeptically. "You say you think someone purposely tried to run her down? Who?"

"That I don't know."

The skepticism on the patrolman's face increased. "Why, then?"

"We're not clear on that point, either."

"Then what makes you think this wasn't just some drunk driving erratically?"

"Not too long ago someone shot her and nearly killed her. I think he was trying to finish the job today."

The policeman's expression became less skeptical and more interested. "You say someone shot her?"

Lisa had rolled down the window a crack to listen. "Contact Detective Overson," she called. "He's working on the case."

"I want to get her away from here as quickly as possible," Slade said with command.

The patrolman nodded. "If your suspicions are true, we'll need some paint scrapings from your car and some photos of the scene. I'll have Jack take you home. You want me to have the car towed somewhere afterward? Looks like the front fender might interfere with driving it."

Lisa gave him the name of her garage. Then with Slade hovering over her like a protective shield, she moved from her car to the police car. Once there, the patrolman contacted Detective Overson.

"He's on his way," the dispatcher informed them after a couple of minutes.

Detective Overson arrived fairly quickly, made a quick appraisal of the scene, then came to stand by the window of the patrol car to speak to Lisa. "Maybe you were the target the first time, but most likely not," he said. "The feds are certain the sniper was a pro. This was definitely amateurish…" He paused then added, "If it even was an attempt on your life. Could have simply been a drunk driver."

"She's nearly been killed twice and you want to write them both off as being in the wrong place at the wrong time?" Slade demanded.

"I don't intend to write either of them off. I was just mentioning the possibility." Overson was an older man with graying hair, dark circles under his eyes and the look of someone who felt he carried the burden of the world on his shoulders. "Damn, if she was the original target this puts us back at square one." His gaze focused on Lisa. "So who wants you dead?"

She shook her head. "I have no idea."

"What cases are you working on?"

Lisa shifted uneasily. "If I open my files to you, then I might as well close shop. People come to me because I'm supposed to be a *private* investigator."

The detective frowned impatiently. "We're talking about your life."

"I know. But my clients aren't going to talk openly to you. Besides, I checked their backgrounds before I accepted their cases. None of them has a criminal record. If I thought I knew which one it was or even had a suspicion, I'd tell you. But I don't. Let me go through my files and I'll get back to you."

Overson didn't look pleased.

"This isn't a game," Slade growled at her. "Turn your files over and let me take you someplace safe until this nut is caught."

"And what if he or she is never caught?" She looked to the detective. "How much time do you have to devote to my case?"

"I've got a pretty heavy caseload," Overson admitted. "But I'll give it priority."

"For about a day or two," she returned. "You'll interview my clients, ruin my chances of ever getting another one, and probably come up with nothing. I'm a trained police officer. I was on the Lubbock force before I came here. The minute I even think I've got a whiff of a suspect, I'll contact you."

"I don't like it. I could get a court order. If someone is after you, you're hindering my investigation."

"And I'll tell the judge that you don't even honestly believe someone is after me...that you're invading my privacy and the privacy of my clients on a fishing expedition when you don't even think there is a fish to be caught."

He didn't refute her words. After a long moment he said, "We'll collect what evidence we can here just in case someone is after you. As for the shooting incident, everything points to it being a mob hit. Truth is, we turned that investigation over to the federal task force. They wanted it and, like I said, we're overworked as it is. But I'll take another look at the evidence."

Slade wanted to insist that Lisa turn her files over to the police, but he knew from the look in her eyes that she was determined to investigate this herself. He also couldn't fault her reasoning. The police would take a look, but if they couldn't come up with a suspect right away, her case would go on the back burner.

The detective started to walk away, hesitated, then returned. "In case I'm wrong and you're right, you take care of yourself. Watch your back."

"I'll be doing that," Slade assured him.

Overson nodded and walked away.

Lisa sat quietly. She had her own plans for how to handle this situation, but this was not the time or place to confront Slade.

"So who wants to kill you?" Slade asked as they were being driven away from the scene.

Lisa gave him a wry look. "Don't you think I would have told Detective Overson if I knew."

"As I recall, you were always a stickler for detail. Even if you had a suspicion, you'd wait until you had proof before you would name anyone. That was a dangerous game then and it's a doubly dangerous game now."

"I have never liked putting innocent people on the hot seat."

"So you do have someone in mind?" he persisted, studying her narrowly.

She breathed a frustrated sigh. "No. I honestly have no clue. I assume it has something to do with one of my cases, but none of them, on the surface, seems that volatile."

"No unhappy clients?"

"Not really."

"Did you uncover some information for a client that might make someone else angry?"

"Could be. There was a divorce case where I found some hidden assets, but that was several months ago."

Another thought struck Slade. "Or maybe it's someone you helped send to jail while you were on the force in Texas."

Lisa's jaw tensed. "Well, whoever it is, they're going to be sorry when I catch up with them."

Slade started to inform her that hell would freeze over before he allowed her to actually go looking for her assailant. But, deciding he didn't want an audience for what he knew would be a heated debate, he chose not to argue with her at that moment.

"What happened?" Helen demanded, rushing out of the house as the police car pulled into the driveway and Lisa and Slade climbed out.

"Whoever tried to kill her before, tried again," Slade said. "This time he tried to run her down." Just saying the words sent a fresh chill down his spine.

Helen paled. "I thought she was just in the wrong place at the wrong time."

"That's still a possibility." Lisa tried to ease her mother's mind. "This might just have been a drunken driver."

Slade knew she playing down the danger for her mother's sake. Hoping that her family could dissuade her from pursuing an investigation, he said, "You've nearly been killed twice. That's one too many coincidences for me."

Guessing his game, Lisa cast him a hostile glance.

Ignoring her anger, Slade again shielded her with his body as he ushered her into the house.

Ester met them just inside the door.

"Slade seems to think that whoever shot Lisa meant to and that he or she tried to kill her again," Helen informed her sister, then quickly turned her full attention to her daughter. "Did he hurt you?"

"Slade got me out of the way. I'm fine. Just a little shaken," Lisa assured her. "My car's damaged, though."

"Cars can be fixed."

"Pack," Slade ordered. "All of you. You're going to

my mother's ranch. You'll be safe there. I'll have my brother, Jess, set up a guarded perimeter.''

"We can't impose," Helen protested.

"It won't be an imposition. You're going to be family." In the next instant he corrected himself. "You are family."

The thought of her mother, aunt or Andy getting injured in the crossfire, shook Lisa to the core. "Slade's right. You need to be someplace safe until I can find out who's trying to kill me."

Slade's expression became stern. "You're staying at the ranch, too. I'll find out who's trying to kill you."

Lisa straightened into a stance of rigid resolve. "Wherever I am, I'll be a target and anyone in my vicinity could get hurt. Besides, this is my battle. The only reason I came to you was to make certain Andy would be taken care of."

Slade faced her with matching resolve. "And I can't think of anything that would be more important for his sake than keeping his mother alive."

Worry etched itself into Helen Gray's face. "I would feel better if you stayed with us and let Slade and the police handle this."

"I'm going to handle this on my own." Lisa glared at Slade. "And I do mean 'on my own.' You're my backup plan for Andy's future."

Slade scowled. "You don't honestly think I'm going to leave you here on your own?"

"If you don't let him stay with you, then I'm staying," Ester interjected. "I may be old and not able to move as fast as I once did, but I'm spry for my age and my eyesight is good."

Slade read the seriousness on Ester's face. His gaze leveled on Lisa. "It's your choice. Me or your aunt."

Lisa knew it would be reckless to go out on her own. Still, she didn't like the idea of putting Slade's life in danger for her sake. But she knew her aunt. Ester meant what she said. That left Lisa with no choice. "Okay, you win."

Slade maintained a cool facade. Inside he grinned. He'd caught the glint of accomplishment in Ester's eyes. Lisa's aunt was a lot like his great-grandmother, Morning Hawk. She knew just how to manipulate people into getting what she wanted. His inward grin vanished as he suddenly pictured Ester and Morning Hawk banded together. None of the rest of the family would stand a chance.

Chapter Four

Lisa hugged Andy tightly. "You be a good boy," she told him.

He nodded. "Goo-od." A plea spread over his face. "Co-ome?"

"I have to stay here for a while." She gave him another tight hug and nuzzled his neck.

"I'll look after your mother, little guy," Slade vowed.

Andy cocked his head in Slade's direction and smiled. "Daa," he said in a voice that left no doubt he considered Slade a friend.

The word wove through Slade like a tender touch. He'd accepted Andy into his heart the moment he'd seen him. That the boy had accepted him filled him with joy. "How about a goodbye hug?" he coaxed, holding out his arms.

Andy glanced toward his mother as if still feeling a need for her guidance, then abruptly deciding he needed none, he held his arms out to Slade.

"I'll protect you and your mother with my life," he vowed gruffly, lifting the boy into his arms.

Andy gave him a lopsided grin then wrapped his arms around Slade's neck and hugged him tightly.

A sharp jab of pain pierced Lisa. She was happy for Andy that he'd found his way into Slade's heart, but at the same time she was hurt that she had never been allowed in. *Warts* she cursed silently. She'd promised herself that she would not feel any more pain where this man was concerned. *And I won't.* Determinedly she shoved the unwanted emotion from her mind.

Ester opened the front door. "The taxi driver is going to get impatient."

Helen gave Lisa a hug. "You take care of yourself." In a fretful voice, she added, "I wish you were coming with us."

Ester had passed through the door and was on the porch. Looking back, she nodded in agreement. "Maybe you should come along and let the police handle this."

"They have no clues and I can't even point them in the right direction," Lisa replied. "Trust me. This is the only way."

Both women looked uncomfortable taking her at her word, but they gave up their protests.

"Stay inside," Slade ordered Lisa, picking up Andy's suitcase and carrying it and the boy outside.

"If I am being watched, I want whoever is after me to know that I'm not going with my family," she said, refusing to obey and stepping out onto the porch to wave goodbye.

Slade picked up his pace, calling out to the driver to come get the rest of the luggage. Reaching the vehicle, he handed Andy over to Helen, then hurried back to Lisa. "Okay. Anyone watching has had a good look. No sense in giving them any more of a shot.'' Slipping an arm around her waist, he nearly lifted her off her feet as he guided her back inside.

Having him so near caused her to feel incredibly secure. Anger that he had that effect on her swept through her. Under normal circumstances he would never have come back into her life. The moment they were inside, she freed herself from his hold and hurried to a window to wave a last goodbye to her family.

Slade caught her by the wrist and pulled her out of view. ''You've got to stop making yourself an easy target.''

Again freeing herself from his hold, a sudden thought occurred to her. ''I've been an easy target many times since the first shooting. And Detective Overson was right about today's attempt being amateurish.'' She shook her head in frustration. ''None of this makes any sense.''

''Well, I'm not buying the 'being in the wrong place at the wrong time' theory,'' Slade said. ''At least, not until we've checked out every possibility.''

''That brings me to the next thing on my agenda.'' Lisa faced him with firm authority. ''You're off this case. I only agreed to let you stay because of my aunt. She can be stubborn. But now that she's gone, I want you to go, as well.''

''Sorry, but you're stuck with me.''

Looking at him standing like an immovable mountain in front of her, Lisa could only think of how large a target he would be. ''If someone is after me, you could get hurt in the crossfire. That wouldn't serve the purpose for which I brought you into this in the first place.''

''If I leave and you get yourself killed, I'd never be able to look our son in the eye again.'' His voice took on an even harsher note. ''I'd never be able to look myself in the eye again.'' Turning on his heels, he headed up the stairs. "Pack a bag. When we leave here, we're not coming back. We'll stay on the move. Whoever is after you might think it's time to step up their attempts on your life. No sense in making you easy prey.'' The set of his jaw told her that arguing would be useless.

She was throwing things into a suitcase when he came into her room. Her eyes rounded in surprise. He was wearing his gun housed in its leather shoulder holster and his badge was pinned on his shirt. "Where'd those come from?"

"Force of habit. I'm so used to traveling on business, I just shoved them in my satchel without thinking about it. Good thing I did."

Lisa couldn't argue with that. Finishing her packing, she went to her closet, took down a locked box, opened it, took out her gun and shoved it into her purse. "All right, let's go."

Picking up her suitcase, Slade carried it downstairs along with his. At the front door he stopped. "You wait here. After I've loaded the luggage into your mother's car and gotten the engine started, I'll come back for you."

She frowned. "I'm not letting you act as a human shield. You get the engine started and I'll come out."

"I don't like it."

"I'll move fast." Seeing the resistance on his face, she added, "Otherwise, I'm going out that door right now and help you load everything into the car."

"Stubborn as a mule," Slade mumbled under his breath. Then with a final scowl of disapproval, he strode outside.

Lisa watched from the door. When he started the engine, she came out of the house and, moving swiftly, climbed into the car.

"Slide down in your seat," he ordered.

Obeying, Lisa had to admit she was glad he was along for the ride. In the next instant she was angry with herself for feeling that way. She would never forgive herself if he was hurt because of her. When she'd gone to him seeking security for her son, she'd never planned on any of this. Studying his taut profile, she wondered how much he was regretting ever inviting her into his life. *A whole lot,* she surmised.

From her house, they drove to her office. Slade parked in the back and insisted on her staying in the car until he unlocked the office door.

Not wanting to give him an opportunity to come back to escort her inside, as soon as she saw it was open, she left the car and hurried inside. Once in the office, they kept the blinds closed so that anyone on the outside would not have a view of them and began reviewing her cases for suspects.

"Since the first attack was only three weeks ago, my guess is that whoever is doing this is involved in one of my more recent investigations. But just to be on the safe side, I think I should consider anything in the past six months," she said, opening a file drawer and sorting through it.

Recalling the other possibility he'd thought of, Slade picked up the phone and punched in a number. "I'll have Boyd check your record back in Texas to see if any felon who might hold a grudge against you has been recently released."

Lisa nodded and continued to pull files and toss them onto her desk in stacks according to the type of investigation.

"Looks like you've been busy," Slade noted as he hung up.

"My aunt knows a lot of people and she was very vocal about promoting me as honest and reliable. The sons of a couple of her friends are members of law firms here and they gave me a chance to prove myself. When I did, they also began to recommend me." She frowned at the stacks of cases. "Mostly, I've worked on simple stuff, nonviolent situations."

She opened two file drawers, each labeled with the name of a law firm. "This is the work I've done this year for them." Her gaze scanned the tabs. "It mostly involved serving subpoenas, divorce papers, et cetera. Nearly everyone in here was a one-time contact."

"Yes, but it was a contact that could change a life," Slade noted.

"True," she conceded. "But you'd think they'd go after the lawyer before they'd go after me. Most of them wouldn't even know who I was. I didn't identify myself. I simply made certain I had the right person and handed them the paper."

"I'd say we could discount those, then. At least for now."

Lisa started to agree, then stopped herself. "Except for two. In those cases I was more involved than just serving subpoenas." She pulled a folder from the top drawer. "In this case it'd be the person who was being testified against, a Mr. Randal Grady, who could be holding a grudge. He'd killed a child while driving drunk. The boy was crossing the street when Grady ran him down...didn't even put his brakes on. But Grady had money, got himself a top-notch lawyer and got off with a couple of months probation and a fine. The boy's parents decided to sue him in civil court, not for the money but because they felt justice hadn't been done.

"Rowanda Gleat was Grady's girlfriend. During his criminal trial, she testified that he'd been drunk that night and he'd been driving the car that struck the boy. She'd also said that the next morning when he realized what he'd done, he was stricken with grief but hadn't gone to the police because he was afraid of the consequences. One of the law firms I work for was handling the case for the parents. When I interviewed Rowanda, there was something about her manner that didn't sit right with me. She reminded me of the cat who'd eaten the canary. At first I attributed that to the huge diamond on her finger. It was, she told me, from Grady. According to her, they were going to get married as soon as the second trial was over. I couldn't stop myself from telling her that I didn't think he was such great husband material. She told me that he'd stay in line for her. There was just something about the way she said it…she was so positive. No one can be that positive about a man like that. I was sure there was something she wasn't telling me. It was just a gut instinct, but a strong one."

"Your gut instincts were always good," Slade noted.

Except where you were concerned, she corrected mentally. She'd been so sure he would learn to care for her. Jerking her mind back to the business at hand, she continued. "I decided to see if I could come up with something to rattle her cage. And I did. Grady had another girlfriend he was treating a whole lot better than Rowanda. I decided to stir up the waters by telling Rowanda about her. The woman blew up. At first she refused to believe me, then when I produced pictures, she swore under her breath—she could have made a sailor blush.

She ended by saying Grady would be sorry, then she threw me out.

"That night she showed up at the new girlfriend's apartment while Grady was there. I was outside in the stairwell across from the apartment door waiting for the brawl I was certain would take place, but it didn't. Grady just looked her in the eye, said, 'Hock the diamond and get out of town or you're dead,' then closed the door in her face.

"Rowanda had turned ashen when he'd threatened her. I thought she might faint. But when he slammed the door in her face, her cheeks were suddenly flaming red. As soon as she got back to her car, I got a call from her on my cell phone. She said that she had information that would burn Grady." Lisa smiled dryly. "He should never have underestimated a woman's scorn."

"So what did she know?"

"She testified that Grady had told her how exhilarating it had been to run down the boy. Her words were, 'He got a real high out of it.' She'd also insisted the attorneys ask her why she hadn't testified to that in the first trial. That gave her the opportunity to tell the world that he'd threatened to kill her. Of course, she made it sound as if he'd done that before the first trial and not just a couple of weeks earlier. It was an interesting courtroom scene. She rose from her chair, pointed a finger at him and said, 'If I'm found dead, I want everyone here to know who was responsible.' His attorneys tried to make it look as if she was merely trying to get even with him for dumping her, but she flashed around that huge diamond ring to show how he'd tried to buy her silence with both money and threats. And the jury preferred her story to his."

"So you think he might be seeking revenge?"

"It's possible. He had a mean temper and the court awarded the parents a tremendous settlement."

"What about the other case?"

Lisa set aside Rowanda's file and pulled a file from the second drawer. "This was a civil action against a plastic surgeon who was a real butcher. One of the witnesses the client wanted subpoenaed was Rachel Miller. She'd been one of the doctor's clients and had ended up with scars and a mishapened nose. She was very self-conscious about her looks and didn't want to appear in public. After I tracked her down, she chose to testify instead of spending time in jail for contempt, but she wasn't happy about the exposure."

Slade turned his attention to one of the stacks of folders on her desk. "And what about these?"

"Two are divorce investigations. I finished one over four months ago and the other three months ago, but the party being investigated might have recently discovered I'd been on their tail."

"And the third?"

"A groom who wants a background check before he ties the knot. He thinks there's something in his fiancée's past she isn't telling him. I was working on that one when I was shot, but hadn't turned up anything."

"And this second stack?"

"They're all background checks on applicants for a CEO position with R.H.T.P. Inc."

"R.H.T.P.?"

"Resolutions for High Tech Problems. It's a computer software and hardware company."

"Might as well start with Rowanda. If Grady is our man, he's sure to be after her, too. And if he hasn't caught up with her, she should be warned she could be in danger."

"I don't know where she is. In spite of her bravado, she was scared of him. She left town right after the trial."

"Then we'll pay a visit to Mr. Grady." Slade tossed all the files she'd pulled into a box and motioned toward the door.

Outside it was dark. Lisa glanced at her watch. "It's late. I suggest we go by his home." She began paging through the file. "I have his address. That's where I tracked Rowanda down the first time."

"We'll take a roundabout route, make certain we're not being tailed," Slade said as they pulled out of their parking space.

Lisa nodded and began giving directions. Once they were satisfied they weren't being followed, she guided him to Grady's residence. It was in one of the more exclusive areas on the outskirts of Seattle. A high iron fence encircled his estate and there was a tall iron gate across the driveway. The gate was closed and locked, barring their entrance, and the house beyond was dark.

Slade pressed the button on the intercom housed in a box on his side of the drive. He got no response. "Looks like he's not home. So what are his favorite hangouts?"

Lisa shifted into a more straightened position in an effort to focus her tired mind. Every muscle in her body screamed in protest. "I'm too tired to go looking for him tonight," she confessed. Her stomach growled and she added, "And I'm hungry."

Mentally, Slade kicked himself for not remembering that she was still recovering from being shot. "We'll call it a day."

A short while later, against Lisa's wishes, Slade had checked them into one of the best hotels in Seattle.

"You're exhausted. I want a place with room service

and a great kitchen. And I can afford it," he'd said, refusing to listen to any argument from her.

Lisa was aware that oil had been struck on the Logan
ranch years ago and that Slade's widowed mother had
insisted on her three sons sharing in the newfound wealth.

As they rode up in the mirrored, expensively carpeted
elevator, the unpleasant thought that his family might
think she'd gotten pregnant to get her hands on some of
Slade's wealth crossed her mind. Her chin tightened. If
the accusation that she was gold digger was made, she'd
point out that if that had been her reason, she wouldn't
have gone off on her own and tried to raise the child by
herself. Still, the thought of meeting his mother under
these circumstances made her uneasy. *But that hurdle is
in the future, so just concentrate on the present,* she ordered herself.

Entering the room, Slade waited until the bellhop had
gone, then said, "I tried to get us a suite but they were
all booked."

Her gaze traveled around the beautifully furnished
room. There were two queen-size beds. "At least one of
us won't be sleeping in a chair. I'll take the bed closest
to the wall. You can sleep in the other one."

Slade nodded his acceptance. But deep inside, he
found himself regretting sleeping alone. Until she'd
walked back into his life, he hadn't realized how much
he'd missed intimate female companionship. Since she'd
left, no other woman had caught his interest. He'd told
himself it was better that way. Women only complicated
a man's life. But seeing Lisa again, he could not deny
that the physical attraction he'd felt toward her was as
strong as ever. Determinedly ignoring the igniting embers
of desire, he picked up the room service menu and
handed it to her. "What do you want to eat?"

Lisa experienced a stab of hurt that he'd accepted the line she'd drawn so easily. *It's what I want,* she reminded herself curtly. Taking the menu, she perused it, told him she wanted the baked chicken, then headed into the bathroom for a hot shower.

The water revived her a little. And she noted that she'd managed to survive her fall to the ground with no noticeable bruising.

"Nice place," she murmured as she finished drying herself and pulled on the heavy terry-cloth robe provided by the hotel. "Very nice place." The thought that it would be perfect for a romantic getaway crossed her mind. Immediately she shoved it out. Letting "romance" and "Slade" mingle together in the same space was not only foolish but stupid.

Leaving the bathroom, she discovered that dinner hadn't arrived. A glance at the clock told her that her family should have arrived at the Logan ranch. "I want to call your mother's place and make certain my family arrived safely."

"I was just waiting for you to get out of the shower," Slade replied, already punching in the number. When the phone began to ring, he handed the receiver to Lisa.

A woman answered.

"This is Lisa, I'd like to speak to my mother," Lisa said after the initial polite exchange of hellos.

"This is Katrina," the woman on the other end identified herself. "Just a second."

Lisa heard Katrina asking someone to tell Helen that her daughter was calling, then Katrina came back on the line. There was laughter in her voice as she said, "I've got someone here who wants to say hello."

Andy's babble sounded from the other end of the line

and Lisa's heart filled with joy. "Are you having a good time?" she asked.

Andy's response was a jumble, but she could hear the excitement in his voice and knew he was all right.

"Your mother's here," Katrina's voice again came over the line. "But I just have to tell you what a darling son you have. He's already stolen everyone's heart."

Lisa was glad for Andy's sake that he was a hit with the family, but she was concerned about her mother and aunt. "How is everything?" she asked as soon as Helen took over the receiver.

"Everyone is being very gracious," Helen replied.

"Are you being honest with me?" Lisa demanded. "I don't want you staying where you're uncomfortable."

"No. Really. And they have all accepted Andy into the fold without any reservations." Her voice softened. "He's finally yawning like crazy. Maybe now that he's heard your voice, I can get him to bed."

"Give him a hug for me," Lisa said. Out of the corner of her eye, she saw Slade motioning that he wanted to talk. "I'm putting Slade on the line. I love you, and give Aunt Ester a hug for me, too."

Handing the phone over to Slade, she heard him ask to speak to Andy and watched as the grim lines of his face softened. When he finished talking to his son, he asked to speak to his mother.

"Are you making our guests comfortable?" he asked bluntly.

Lisa heard the indignant "Of course" from where she stood.

The grimness had returned to Slade's face. "What I really meant was, is Morning Hawk behaving herself?"

Lisa knew Morning Hawk was Slade's great-grandmother. She also knew that the elderly Apache made Slade uneasy at times. She was, he'd said once, unpredictable and overly blunt. When Slade's expression relaxed somewhat, Lisa guessed that his mother had assured him that Morning Hawk was behaving herself and for her family's sake, Lisa was glad.

Next, Slade asked to speak to Jess, his younger brother, who, Lisa knew, ran the ranch for his mother.

From Slade's side of the conversation, she gathered that Jess had set up the protective perimeter. Knowing her family was safe, she stretched out on the bed and allowed herself to relax.

When Slade hung up, she turned on the television. She was too tired to make small talk and, for a short while at least, she didn't want to think about who was trying to kill her.

"Think I'll wash up, too," Slade said, heading into the bathroom.

Lisa tried to ignore his presence by concentrating on the movie on the TV screen, but, in her tired state, her eyelids grew heavier and closed over her eyes. The sound of the shower took precedence over all other noises in the room and her inner vision was filled with the image of her and Slade bathing together. Her jaw firmed in self-directed irritation. Opening her eyes, she pushed the image from her mind. She'd never thought of herself as the affair type. And she wasn't, really. Slade had been the only man she'd ever shared a bed with. And she hadn't planned on doing that. But the attraction had been too strong.

A bitter smile curled up one corner of her mouth. Besides, she'd been certain she could break down the barriers he'd kept around his heart and that one day he'd marry her. By the time she accepted the fact that she wasn't going to succeed, Andy was on the way.

* * *

In the shower, his voice masked by the running water, Slade cursed under his breath. He'd known she was wearing nothing under the terry-cloth robe and had needed no imagination to picture her without it. He remembered every inch of her in vivid detail. Why couldn't she be more practical and accept the fact that physically they were a great match and not demand any more?

Returning to the room, a question that had been on his mind insisted on being asked. "Since you didn't want a life with me, why didn't you get an abortion?"

Lisa opened her eyes and met his gaze. "I didn't want a life with you *and your ghost*," she corrected. "And I still don't," she added pointedly. "As for the abortion, from the moment I discovered I was pregnant, my baby was a real person to me. And, maybe, I wanted a piece of you that Claudette didn't possess." Mentally she kicked herself. She hadn't meant to be so open about her feelings, but she'd been holding too much inside for too long and in her tired state, it was escaping. She sat up, her shoulders squared with pride. "I realize that given the choice you would have preferred that he'd never been born."

Slade's gaze leveled on her. "No. I wouldn't have wanted that. What I would have wanted, was to have known the truth from the beginning so that I could have been there when he was born."

"I did what I thought was best," she returned through clenched teeth.

Slade grimaced as if angry with himself. "Sorry, I don't want to argue with you. I understand why you did what you did." His tone took on a terse plea. "But now that I know about Andy, I want to be a full-time father. I'm asking you to give our marriage a chance to work."

"Marriage should be built on a foundation of love."

His jaw hardened. "Very successful ones are built on a foundation of friendship and respect. And, we already know we're physically compatible. I just want you to think about it."

In her mind's eye, Lisa could see Claudette standing beside him, her arm curled possessively around his. "No. I'll marry you and I'll allow Andy's name to be changed to Logan, and I'll sign all the papers necessary to make him legally your son, but I will never consider ours a real marriage and I won't stay married to you after all the legalities have been completed."

Slade considered trying to change her mind, but she would always want more than he was willing to give. "If that's the way you want it, then that's how it will be."

Lisa's stomach knotted and she realized she'd hoped he would give her some reason to believe that if she agreed to try to make their marriage work, he might allow her past the barriers and into his heart.

He wouldn't let you in before, a small voice chided her. *You were an idiot to even consider the possibility he'd change even for his son's sake.*

To her relief, the food arrived at that moment.

Almost too tired to eat, Lisa didn't even try to make conversation. She ate, then crawled under the covers and went to sleep.

Slade continued to sit in his chair. Watching her as she slept, he felt an emptiness and knew that if he let down his guard, she could fill the void within him. He forced the image of his late wife to the forefront of his mind. The pain was stronger than the emptiness. Pulling his gaze away from Lisa, he, too, went to bed.

Chapter Five

Slade woke early the next morning. Seeing Lisa snuggled into her covers with her face nearly buried in her pillow brought back a fresh flood of memories of waking with her. Before he was in need of a cold shower, he rose and dressed.

Lisa had been feigning sleep. Opening her eyes just a crack as he rose, she felt her whole body flame at the sight of him. She was well aware that he preferred to sleep in the nude, but this morning he was wearing jockey shorts. She guessed this bit of modesty was out of courtesy to her. But in her mind's eye she visualized him without them and the heat became even hotter. The temptation to give in to his wishes and to be a wife to him blossomed into life. *He'll never feel anything deeper than lust for you.* She pushed the thought from her mind.

She waited until he'd gone into the bathroom, then rose and hurriedly dressed. The sooner they were out of this room the better. Even after all she'd been through with him, the lust he evoked in her was close to overwhelming.

"Thought we'd get some breakfast from a fast-food place on our way to Grady's," she said when Slade came back into the room. "I'd like to catch him before he heads out to his office."

For a long moment Slade stood, his gaze traveling over her, and Lisa saw that morning lust look in his eyes. Then his expression became shuttered. "Right," he said, and continued past her to retrieve his holstered gun.

The realization that if he'd touched her, there was a strong possibility her resistance would have crumbled and she would have gone into his arms shook her to the core. *Don't you dare weaken,* she ordered herself, and continued on into the bathroom to splash cold water on her face.

A short while later she and Slade were back at Grady's house. Slade pressed the intercom button but again received no response.

"Nobody's home," a male voice called.

Lisa looked to the sidewalk and saw a man with a Great Dane on a leash, obviously out for a morning stroll. Climbing out of the car, she gave him her best smile. "We're looking for Mr. Grady."

Slade had climbed out of the car and the man's gaze shifted to him. "You don't look like local law enforcement," he said, coming closer for a better view of the badge Slade was wearing. "Texas Ranger." He shook his head. "I'm not surprised. So what'd he do down there?"

"He's not wanted for anything. We just need to talk to him," Slade said in an easy drawl.

"Well, you're too late. He got himself into another

traffic accident about two months ago. This time, he managed to kill himself. Good riddance, if you ask me."

Slade extended his hand to the man. "Thanks for the information."

The man accepted the handshake, nodded to Lisa, then continued on down the street.

"That takes care of Grady," Lisa said, opening the back passenger door and tossing the file onto the seat.

"So which case do you want to look into next?" Slade asked.

"Rachel Miller." Lisa pulled the woman's file out of the box, closed the door and climbed into the front seat. "The more I think about it, the more she seems like a likely candidate to go off the deep end. She was very high-strung."

Slade drove to the address she gave him. It was a split-level home in one of the more upscale suburbs. The large front lawn was beautifully manicured and the gardens were full of flowers. "This place has taken on a new life," Lisa remarked, recalling how the lawn had been in desperate need of a mowing and the gardens had been inundated with weeds on her first trip here. "The place used to look as depressed as its owner was. Maybe she moved."

"Don't let your guard down just because the scenery is prettier," Slade ordered.

Lisa frowned at herself for being distracted by the change in the place. Still, she was ready to wager that Rachel Miller didn't live here anymore. *And I would have lost that wager,* she admitted when their knock was answered by the small brunette. It was the same Rachel Miller but different. She was all smiles and there was an expression of honest welcome on her face.

"Miss Gray," the woman gushed, recognizing Lisa immediately. "It's so good to see you again."

Slade glanced at Lisa questioningly.

Catching the exchange, Rachel laughed. "I'll admit we parted under less friendly circumstances, but I owe everything to Miss Gray." She made a large waving gesture with her arm to indicate their surroundings. Her expression becoming sympathetic, she returned her attention to Lisa. "I was so sorry to read about you getting shot."

"Thanks." Lisa was having a hard time getting used to the new Rachel Miller and couldn't help wondering if this was an act. But it didn't look or feel like an act.

"Oh, my manners," Rachel admonished herself. "Please, come in. Can I offer you some coffee?"

"No, thanks," Lisa replied for both herself and Slade as they stepped inside. In the hall, there was a huge mirror on the wall and a bouquet of flowers on the table beneath it. And there was a light and airy feel to the house. The last time she'd been here, the curtains had all been drawn and there had been no mirror.

Rachel led the way into the living room. When they were all seated, she regarded Lisa with a puzzled look. "I'm glad to see you so that I can thank you, but why are you here?"

"We think that Lisa wasn't shot by accident. We think she might have been the target," Slade said bluntly.

For a moment Rachel said nothing, then her smile returned. "And you thought I might be responsible."

"You were very upset with me," Lisa reminded her.

Rachel nodded. "You're right. I was." Her expression became one of gratitude. "But I'm not angry with you any longer. I owe this whole new life to you." Excitement spread over her features. "I've been on television." She named several of the most popular talk shows and two morning news shows. "They all wanted to do something to warn people about plastic surgery…you know, how to really be careful about choosing a doctor and not expecting too much." Her smile broadened. "And next week, I'm going in for some reconstructive surgery by the very best plastic surgeon in the country. He does all the Hollywood stars. And it's not even going to cost me anything. It's going to be one of those before-and-after bits."

With a laugh of pure pleasure, Rachel added, "I've even got a booking agent. He specializes in people with unique situations. I'll bet he could find spots for a female detective. Do you want his name and number?"

"Thanks, but no thanks." Lisa mentally crossed Rachel off her list of suspects.

The woman shrugged and turned her attention to Slade. "I'm sure he could find spots for you."

Lisa scowled. The woman was practically drooling. "Thanks, but no thanks for him, as well," she answered for Slade. Irked by this flash of jealously, she rose. "We need to be going."

Following her lead, Slade rose, also. "We appreciate your time."

"It's been my pleasure," Rachel assured him, her voice near a purr as she rose and accompanied them to the door.

Again Lisa experienced a jab of jealousy. The temptation to inform Rachel Miller that Slade was her fiancé suddenly surfaced. *Claiming Slade for my own would be an act of lunacy,* she conceded to herself. *He belongs to Claudette and his fear of losing a woman he loves is going to keep him committed to her.* The flash of jealousy quelled, she nodded a final goodbye to Rachel and exited the house.

turn

Li

"I wa

Dist

nicely

realized

"Henry

and opene

wanted his

Silently c

stop lusting a

ness.

"If Isabelle

her past and she   ne might

have wanted me

If Isabelle Montgomery doesn't know sh

doesn't want her finding

vestigated, I don't want Henry down

They tracked Henry down

see you back on your feet

and rounding it to sh

ing his hand to Sla

"Something

It was c

he'd b

sw

72

Slade paged th   ...es in the folder. "There
doesn't appear to b anything suspicious in here."

"No. But that's just a surface check…education,
names and addresses of close family members, job history, any past police record, the kind of stuff you can
find with a computer or telephone. In addition, he'd requested a full month's surveillance and a more in-depth
look into her family history with short bios on her
mother, father and their parents. I was just getting ready
to start on all of that when I got shot and the case got
put on hold. At least, as far as I know it did. Could be
he found another investigator to take over. I suggested
Amy Jacob and her father. We've worked together oc-
casionally. But when they came to visit me in the hospital, they said he hadn't called."

"So who do we go see first…the client or the fiancée?"

"The client. My work is supposed to be confidential.

e was being in-
ut from me."

at his office. "I'm glad to
," he said, rising from his desk
ke hands with Lisa. Then, extend-
de, he grinned. "You her bodyguard?"
g like that."

ear from the change in Henry's expression that
en joking about the bodyguard business. His gaze
ung back to Lisa. "I thought the papers said you were
shot by accident. That it was that hood that was the real
target."

"Could be the police were wrong about that," Slade
said.

Henry's gaze returned to him and fixed on Slade's
badge. "You're a Texas Ranger. I've always wanted to
meet one of you guys. But how'd you get involved?"

"He's an old friend," Lisa said, finding it impossible
to refer to Slade as her fiancé. Even "friend" didn't taste
right on her tongue. He was a brain-muddler. That was
what he was! Realizing that Slade had garnered all of her
thoughts again, she curtly jerked her mind back to the
reason they were there. "We're interested in knowing
what the current situation is with your fiancée."

Henry shrugged. "It's over. She's gone."

"Gone?" Lisa's tone coaxed him to elaborate.

"Isabelle wanted to set the wedding date. I wanted to
put it off until you could finish your investigation. I felt
pressured so I told my best friend about hiring you. He
told his girlfriend who just happens to not like Isabelle
and she couldn't wait to tell her. Isabelle called me and
asked if it was true. I decided not to lie and told her that
it was. The next thing I knew, I got a special delivery

package with my ring in it and a note with one word—
goodbye.''

Henry motioned for them to be seated, then headed
back around his desk and seated himself. "I thought
about it and decided she had a right to get mad. I gave
her a day to cool off, then went to her place to see if we
could patch things up. Her roommate said she'd used her
vacation time for the two week notification to quit her
job and gone back home to Ohio.''

"When was that?''

Henry frowned thoughtfully for a moment, then said,
"It was just before you were shot. I was going to call
you and tell you that I didn't need your services any
longer, but I was sort of curious about why she ran so I
figured I'd let you continue the investigation when you
were well. Now, I'm not interested any longer. She's part
of my past and I figure it's best to keep it that way.''

"You haven't tried to contact her?'' Lisa asked, noting
that the man didn't look all that broken-hearted.

"No. Clearly she has something to hide. That makes
her unsuitable wife material. Like I said, at first I was
curious about what had caused her to run, but I've lost
interest. Just send me a bill for services rendered. As far
as I'm concerned, hiring you was well worth the price.''

Thanking Henry for his time, Lisa and Slade left.

"Looks like this Isabelle Montgomery is a very likely
suspect,'' Slade said as they drove away.

Lisa scowled cynically. "And if she isn't the one after
me, she's lucky to be rid of that man. He'd got the staying power of a snowman in July.'' Glancing through the
Ogden folder, she found what she was looking for and
began punching in a number on her cell phone.

"Who are you calling?''

"Her mother lives in Dayton. Figured I'd start there.

If she didn't actually go *home*, then her mother should know where to find her.''

When a woman answered, Lisa introduced herself as someone from the personnel office of the company where Isabelle had worked in Seattle, and asked if she could speak to her.

"I'm her mother. Isabelle is out of town, but I'm expecting her back late tonight," the woman on the other end informed her. "Can I help you?"

Lisa said she was calling about a problem with Isabelle's last paycheck. "It's nothing serious," she assured the woman, then adding that she'd call back the next day, she ended the call. "Looks like she did move back home, but she's been out of town lately. It's beginning to look more and more like she could be the one we're after." Frowning thoughtfully, she added, "Only, Margaret Montgomery didn't seem the least bit worried about someone trying to contact her daughter."

"So maybe she doesn't know her daughter has anything to hide."

Lisa nodded in agreement.

"Next stop, Dayton, Ohio," Slade said. "Which way to the airport?"

Lisa considered protesting about the amount of money Slade was spending to help her find her would-be killer, but bit back the words. He would only give her an indulgent look and tell her that he was doing his duty by her. Besides, she wanted to find her pursuer as quickly as possible so she could be with her son again.

A while later, as the plane taxied down the runway, Lisa sat back in her seat and closed her eyes. Slade had called Detective Overson from the airport to find out if the police had discovered anything about the car and driver who'd tried to run her down. Overson informed him that they'd found the car abandoned in a lot on the west side of town. It had been reported stolen the day before the incident by an elderly couple. The only discernable fingerprints on the steering wheel belonged to the elderly woman. In a couple of places the prints were badly smudged and the police hypothesized that whoever had stolen the car had worn gloves.

It was late evening when they arrived in Dayton. Both tired, they opted to grab dinner at a fast-food restaurant, then checked into the first respectable-looking motel they saw. As soon as they settled in their room, Lisa called the ranch to check on her family.

It was earlier in Texas and she heard Andy laughing in the background when Slade's mother answered the phone.

His voice grew nearer as her mother came to the phone and the longing to hold him in her arms grew intense. "There's someone here who wants to talk to you," Helen said, laughter in her voice.

"Pon-ney. Meee. Ri-idee," the toddler garbled excitedly when Helen put him on the phone. "Coowbooy. Meee."

Lisa hadn't ridden since she was in her early teens, and the mother in her panicked. Andy was just a toddler. His legs wouldn't even reach around a pony. Her mind flashed back to the times she'd fallen. There had only been two and she hadn't been injured except for her pride and a small amount of bruising, still the possibility of serious injury had existed. Not wanting to alarm Andy, she hid her concern until her mother came back on the line.

"They have a child-size saddle and Andy's only allowed to ride in the corral with Jess walking on one side keeping a hand on him while one of the ranch hands walks on the other,'' Helen assured her.

Still, Lisa remained apprehensive.

When she handed the phone to Slade, he spoke first to Andy and then to Jess. As he went through a checklist of safety precautions with his brother, Lisa realized that he was as concerned for their son's safety as she was.

"Thanks," she said when he hung up.

Slade raised a questioning eyebrow.

"For making certain Jess was being very careful with Andy," she elaborated.

"He's my son, too. I don't want to see him injured."

She heard the irritation in his voice and knew he was angry with her for thinking he wouldn't be concerned. "I just figured that you'd be so proud Jess was making a cowboy out of him that you wouldn't consider the danger," she said to defend herself. She meant to stop there, but something that had always concerned her about his behavior insisted on being said. "You disregard danger to yourself."

He scowled. "I always know what I'm doing."

"I think that's what used to frighten me most. You did always know what you were doing." Deep inside the pain he'd caused her in the past came back as intense as ever. "I used to wonder if you placed yourself in harm's way because you wanted to join Claudette so badly you were willing to die to accomplish that aim."

"I was just doing my job. That's what lawmen do…put their lives on the line."

She met his gaze. "That time you didn't wait for backup and went in after that drug dealer yourself was putting your life way over the line. Then there was that bank robbery with hostages when you walked right in and offered yourself to the robbers in place of hostages."

"I didn't want the drug dealer getting away. As for the hostages, I figured it was my job to do what I could to save them."

He'd given her the same reasons at the time the incidents had occurred. She hadn't bought them then and she wasn't buying them now. The only difference was, at that time, she hadn't voiced her opinion that Claudette had anything to do with his behavior. She hadn't wanted to accept the fact that Claudette's hold on him was that strong. Frustration swept through her. "You're a stubborn, hardheaded fool, who'd rather live in the past than face the future." Without giving him a chance to respond, she stalked into the bathroom to take a shower.

Slade sat staring at the closed door between them. He recalled how angry she'd been with him following the drug bust. She'd been working on the drug enforcement task force with him and had been in one of the backup units that had responded to his call. When the units arrived and the officers discovered that he had gone in singlehandedly and taken the five people inside into custody, they had accepted his actions without comment. Lisa, on the other hand, had taken him aside and told him just what an idiot she'd thought he was.

That was when he'd asked her out on their first date. He'd liked her spunk. He knew some of the others had to be thinking the same thing, but she had been the only one who'd had the nerve to say it.

He also recalled the very last time they'd spoken before she left Lubbock. He'd been surprised when she'd showed up at his door. She'd been avoiding him since their final date. She'd refused his invitation to come inside. Instead she'd said stiffly, "I've just come by to say something I feel needs to be said. If Claudette loved you as much as you love her, she wouldn't want you throwing away your life by taking unnecessary chances.'' Then she'd walked away and he hadn't seen her again until she'd showed up at his home to tell him about his son.

So maybe he had been a little cavalier about his life, but she was wrong about his motives.

Lisa came out of the bathroom to find Slade where she'd left him.

"I don't have a death wish,'' he said. ''I'll admit that maybe I take risks, but they're always calculated risks. I've always been that way. I was that way when Claudette was alive."

Lisa had heard other officers say that Slade had always been a risk-taker, but she'd assumed that behavior had started after his wife had died. Finding out that Claudette wasn't the reason for his dare-devil behavior was a relief. But it was short-lived. "So you're saying that you were born foolish.''

Slade grinned crookedly. "Guess so.''

He looked so boyishly appealing, her heart skipped a beat. Silently she cursed. She was a practical, level-headed woman. How could she have allowed herself to fall in love with a man who was bound to a ghost and had a reckless streak, as well? *"Being in love'' was in the past,* she assured herself. She'd gotten over him and she would not allow herself to fall back into that dismal pit of pain and frustration.

"And I'm not the only one who took chances.'' Recalling some of her behavior, his expression became serious. "You gave me a few white hairs with some of your antics.''

"I was never as oblivious to danger as you were,'' she returned curtly. Refusing to get into a one-upmanship battle with him, she said a sharp, "Good night,'' then climbed into bed and went to sleep.

Chapter Six

The next morning they knocked on the Montgomerys' door at nine.

A woman who looked to be in her mid-fifties answered.

"I'm Lisa Gray," Lisa introduced herself. "And this is Slade Logan. We need to speak to Miss Isabelle Montgomery."

The woman's gaze focused on Slade's badge. "Why would a Texas Ranger want to speak to my daughter?"

"Mom, who's at the door?" a woman's voice sounded from down the hall. It was accompanied by footsteps coming their way.

"These people want to talk to you," the older woman said as a younger version of herself joined them at the door.

Isabelle's gaze skimmed over Lisa and focused on Slade, traveling from his gun to his badge. "You're a Texas Ranger? What are you doing in Ohio?"

"That's what we'd like to talk to you about," Slade replied in an easy drawl.

"I don't know anybody in Texas."

Lisa moved so that she was between Slade and Isabelle. "I'm a private investigator from Seattle and I was hired by Henry Ogden to investigate you."

Isabelle frowned. "I don't understand. I called off the engagement." Her expression turned dry. "I can't believe he continued to have me investigated."

"He didn't."

"If you've tracked me down to tell me that he's sorry. Forget it."

"That's not why we're here," Slade said.

Isabelle's gaze moved back to his badge. "No. I guess it wouldn't be. Texas Rangers don't usually make house calls for the lovelorn." Suddenly cynical amusement sparkled in her eyes. "So did it turn out that Henry had something to hide?" The amused gleam increased. "It must be something big if the Texas authorities have sent a Ranger all the way to Ohio just to interview me."

"Could we speak in private?" Lisa requested.

"Yes. Sure." Isabelle motioned them inside.

"Would you like some coffee?" Mrs. Montgomery offered.

"No, thanks," both Lisa and Slade spoke in unison.

The woman's lips pursed in an expression of dislike. "I knew that Ogden man was a bad apple. Having my daughter investigated...who did he think he was?" Having had her say, Mrs. Montgomery headed down the hall.

The way Margaret spoke, made it apparent to Lisa that Isabelle had told her mother about Henry hiring a private detective. It was also apparent that Margaret wasn't worried about her daughter having anything to hide. *But then, children don't always tell their parents everything,* she reminded herself.

Isabelle guided them into the living room. "So what kind of trouble is dear Henry in?"

"He's not." It was Lisa who spoke as she and Isabelle seated themselves.

Slade didn't sit. Instead he moved to a corner of the room, a short distance from the women, and leaned against the wall in a relaxed pose.

Lisa knew his easy manner was merely for show.

The amusement Isabelle had been exhibiting vanished as her gaze traveled from Lisa to Slade, then back to Lisa, "What's going on?"

"Someone has tried twice to kill me in the past three weeks," Lisa said bluntly.

Isabelle stared. "Kill you?"

Lisa noted that the woman seemed genuinely stunned.

"I don't understand. Why are you here?" Again the cynical expression returned to her face. "You think Henry had something to do with it?"

"No." It was Slade who spoke.

Shock and fear mingled in Isabelle's features, followed by indignation as her gaze swung back to Lisa. "You can't possibly think I had something to do with that? Why in the world would I want to kill you?"

"You found out I was investigating you and there is something you wanted to make certain I didn't find out."

"That's absurd."

"So where were you..." Lisa named the date of the first attack on her.

"What day of the week was that?"

"Wednesday."

"What time?"

"Ten a.m."

"Then I was at work."

"And where were you two days ago?"

"I was in St. Louis, visiting a friend."

"I'll need the name and address of the friend."

"How dare you come into my house and make such a ridiculous accusation against my daughter." Mrs. Montgomery strode into the room, her face red with rage. Reaching her daughter's side, she wound an arm protectively around the younger woman's shoulders.

Slade straightened into a more alert stance.

Lisa stood her ground. "She left Seattle in a hurry. I want to know why."

"Because the man I thought loved me, didn't trust me."

"People break up all the time. But most don't quit their jobs and move halfway across the country. That requires a very good reason."

"I was disillusioned. I knew his grandmother didn't like me. She didn't think I was good enough for him. When I found out about the investigation, I knew she was the one who'd put him up to it. But what hurt most was that he'd gone along with her. That was when I finally admitted to myself how strong a hold she had on him and I knew she'd make my life miserable if I went through with the wedding. So I decided to call the whole thing off, come home and get a fresh start."

"Considering how easily Mr. Ogden accepted your decision, I'd say you did the right thing." As she spoke Lisa's mind again flashed back to how easily Slade had accepted her departure. The protective shield she'd been erecting around her heart grew stronger.

Slade caught the subtle glance Lisa cast in his direction and knew the wall she was building between them was getting thicker. So maybe that was just as well. If they stayed together, eventually she'd want an emotional commitment and that was something he wasn't willing to give.

"That's exactly right." It was Mrs. Montgomery who spoke. "My daughter is a smart woman with good instincts. She knows when to get out of a bad situation. Besides, I wanted her to come home. I'd been asking her to. Since she left, I've been very lonely."

Lisa's attention jerked to the mother. Something wasn't right. From her arrival here, she'd sensed a closeness between mother and daughter she hadn't expected. Less than six months after her father died, Isabelle had quit a job in Dayton where she'd had a managerial position and moved to Seattle to begin again. Lisa had assumed this was Isabelle's way of breaking away from a mother she didn't get along with. But that didn't seem to be the case. Lisa returned her attention to Isabelle. "So why did you go to Seattle in the first place?"

"I wanted a change of scenery. I felt like my life was in a rut."

Lisa didn't buy that explanation, either. "You could have simply gone on a vacation. It's obvious you and your mother are close. I find it very peculiar that you would up and leave her on her own so soon after your father's death."

Mrs. Montgomery glared at her. "My daughter's reason for going to Seattle was personal. She had nothing to do with any attempts made on your life and that's all you need to know."

"I'd wager the homestead that you and your daughter are hiding something." Slade spoke in an easy drawl, but as soft as it was, it carried a warning to not mess with him. "And, it could be that she had nothing to do with the attempts on Lisa's life. However, if what you're hiding involves someone else, it's possible that person could be responsible. We want the whole truth. Either you tell us, or we'll find out on our own.''

Isabelle's jaw hardened and both women remained mute.

So they are protecting someone. "I'll start with your phone records and talk to everyone you've spoken to in the past year,'' Lisa said.

"I have a right to my privacy,'' Isabelle snapped.

"Not if your 'privacy' involves getting an innocent woman murdered,'' Slade growled.

"I swear to you, my private life had nothing to do with the attempts on Miss Gray,'' Isabelle insisted.

"I have to insist on us being the ones to determine that,'' Slade returned.

A look passed between mother and daughter. They were clearly not happy. Isabelle turned back to Lisa and Slade. "I want your promise that you will keep what I tell you confidential.''

"As long as we are assured it has nothing to do with the attempts on Lisa's life,'' Slade stipulated.

Isabelle continued to hesitate, her discomfort obvious.

In the end, it was Mrs. Montgomery who spoke. "After Peter died, I felt compelled to tell Isabelle the truth. He was so good to me and her that while he was alive it didn't seem right to say anything. She could not have had a better father.'' Mrs. Montgomery fell silent.

"But he wasn't my biological father,'' Isabelle said what her mother was having trouble saying.

Mrs. Montgomery nodded, then her shoulders stiffened defensively. "From the beginning, before we exchanged vows, he knew the truth, but we never told Isabelle. After I saw one of those shows about people who needed to know their true family's medical history, I wrote everything out in a letter to Isabelle and put the letter in my safe-deposit box. Peter knew it was there. If anything had happened to me, he would have given it to her if it had become necessary. She would have found it after we were both gone.'' The mother looked to her daughter. ''I know it would have been a shock under those circumstances, but I really didn't know how else to handle it.''

Isabelle slipped her arm around her mother's waist. ''I understand.''

''So after your husband died, you decided to tell your daughter the truth.'' Lisa brought the conversation back to the point she was most interested in.

Mrs. Montgomery's gaze shifted back to Lisa. ''Yes. Her father was—is a man by the name of Bruce Priceman. He and I were high school sweethearts. The summer after we graduated, we quarreled, he joined the army and left. He'd been gone about a month when I realized I was pregnant. I was working at Peter Montgomery's hardware store. Peter was twenty-five years my senior, widowed with no children. He was the kindest man I ever knew. I couldn't tell my parents. Peter found me crying in the stockroom and I told him. His first suggestion was that I write to Bruce. He was sure Bruce would do the honorable thing. But I had my pride. He hadn't written, called or made any attempt to contact me since he'd left.''

The strain of telling her story was showing on Mrs. Montgomery's face. She sank into a nearby chair. ''Peter's next solution was for me to marry him and let him claim the baby. There was some gossip, but Peter was so proud of Isabelle and so good to me and I did care for him, that the gossip faded and people accepted our marriage as a good thing.''

Again Mrs. Montgomery paused, then continued. ''Bruce came home after a year. He knew about the marriage and the baby and had figured out that Isabelle was probably his. He hadn't come to claim us, he'd only come to make certain we were all right. I suppose he would have taken us with him if we'd been unhappy, but we weren't. And, it was obvious that he was relieved. He even told me so. He said he wasn't prepared to be a father and support a family. I think I knew all along that he wasn't good husband material. His own family was pretty dysfunctional. He and his father fought all the time. I don't think he even went to see them when he was in town. Anyway, after he was assured that I was happy, he left again and, this time, he never came back.''

Her eyes glazed as if the past was filling her vision. "It was all so very civilized. We were all so polite to each other. I suppose I never really loved Bruce. What we had was merely passion…teenage passion at that. To be honest, I was glad to see him go. Peter made me feel safe and secure and loved and, luckily, I had matured enough to realize those were the qualities I really wanted in a marriage.''

Smart woman, Lisa applauded Mrs. Montgomery mentally, wishing she'd found someone to take Slade's place.

Slade caught the look on Lisa's face and guessed what she was thinking. The thought of another man taking his place as husband and father caused a bitter taste in his mouth. Forcing his mind back to the current situation, he focused on Mrs. Montgomery. "And so you never said anything about Bruce Priceman to your daughter until after your husband's death.''

"No. I didn't feel it was fair to Peter. In his heart and in Isabelle's, he was her father and he'd earned the right to be. But after he was gone, I decided the time had come to tell her the truth.''

"And I decided I wanted to meet my real father.''

Isabelle picked up the story. "Or, at least, to find out what had happened to him. I hired a private investigator to find him and to find out about his life. It seems he stayed in the military for twenty years, then retired. He'd been married and divorced once during the time he'd been in service. No children. After he retired, he started working for a computer company in Seattle. He's president of it now and he's married to the founder's daughter."

"You were working for a computer company. Was that his?" Lisa asked.

Isabelle nodded. "Yes. I went to see him. I told him I didn't want anything from him. I just wanted to meet him. He was very kind. As it turned out, he and his second wife hadn't had any children, either, and there is no prospect of them ever having any. She has cancer and is dying. He asked me to stay and learn the business. Apparently, he'd kept up with me and had made me the primary heir in his will. The only thing he asked was that we keep our relationship a secret until his wife passed away. He didn't want her having to face people whispering about him, me and her. He wanted her final days to be peaceful."

"And you were afraid I would uncover the connection and tell Henry?"

"Actually, there was more to it than that." Isabelle perched on the arm of the chair her mother was occupying. "Henry is a very charming man. But like I said, I had begun to worry that he was too influenced by his grandmother. She's a wealthy woman and measures people by their social standing and the amount of their estate...the amount of their estate holding sway over social standing. Basically those were her objections to me. As far as she knew, I had no social status and certainly no fortune. It occurred to me that if she found out about my true parentage and my father's plans for me, her attitude would change. My father is a very wealthy man. And it irked me to think that she really didn't care what kind of person I was, she only cared about what material things I could bring to her family. And I had also begun to have my doubts about Henry's feelings for me. The truth is, I'd begun to wonder if he wasn't more superficial than I'd believed. I knew that if he found out the truth, I'd never be certain about him. So I left. I guess I wanted to see if he would come after me. He didn't, and that gave me my answer.''

"Did you tell your father about the investigation?"

"Yes, but he wouldn't try to murder you. He has no reason to want you dead."

"You said his wife was the owner's daughter. Once a secret is out, it's out. Her finding out about you could cost him his job as well as any inheritance he expected to receive when she died."

Isabelle scowled. "My father is a computer genius. His wife's father was the founder of the company but my father owns nearly all of the patents that make the company profitable."

"He would still be in danger of losing any inheritance he expected to get from his wife," Lisa pointed out. "Money can be a very strong motive."

Isabelle shook her head. "Not in this case. Soon after I left Seattle, my father discovered that his wife, her name's Elaine, thought he'd been having an affair. A *friend* of hers had seen him with me and felt obliged to tell her. Apparently, she'd suffered in silence and it was harming her health. Anyway, she finally told him and he told her about my mother and himself. She said she was glad he wouldn't be alone when she was gone, then she insisted on meeting me and my mother. A couple of weeks ago, we flew to Seattle and met her and her family. They were all kind to us and accepted me graciously.'' A plea spread over her features. ''But they and my mother and I are private people. We were hoping to keep this all in the family, at least for a while. I know eventually other people will learn the truth, but we'd like some time to adjust before it becomes public knowledge.''

''I understand,'' Lisa said. ''We won't divulge your secret.''

Relief spread over Isabelle's face. ''Thanks.'' A cynical spark of amusement suddenly twinkled in her eyes. ''I would like to be a fly on the wall when Henry's grandmother finds out.''

Lisa nodded.

Slade tried to concentrate on the facts of the case as they drove back to the airport, but the vision of Lisa and Andy being loved and cared for by another man continued to haunt him. He told himself this was because he wanted to be Andy's full-time father...not only did he care for the boy, but it was his duty and his obligation. And he knew he would take better care of both of his son and Lisa than anyone else ever would. Abruptly, he said, ''I can provide you and Andy with financial security and I'll take care of the both of you to the utmost of my ability. We can have as good a life as Mrs. Montgomery had with her husband.''

Lisa continued to stare out the front windshield at the road ahead. She couldn't deny she was tempted. But... ''I want more.'' Her words seemed to echo in the car. They were followed by a deafening silence; neither said anything more until they reached the airport.

There they discovered they couldn't get a flight out until the next day.

"I could use some lunch and then some rest," Lisa said.

A while later they'd eaten and checked into a nearby motel. As soon as they'd entered the room, Lisa had crawled into bed and gone to sleep.

Now, Slade sat in a chair, the folder containing the names of the job applicants she'd researched open on the table in front of him. But his gaze was on her. Being with her made him feel good and that feeling caused a twist of guilt. The image of his late wife Claudette came vividly back. He pushed it out of his mind and forced himself to concentrate on the information in the folder.

By the time Lisa woke from her nap, Slade had managed to get locations on all of the candidates and their current job status. Two had been hired by the company she'd worked for. Five had found good positions elsewhere and the eighth had started his own business in New York.

Another possibility had occurred to Slade. He waited until she'd fully wakened and joined him at the table.

"Have you found anything that might lead us to the right suspect?" she asked.

"None of the men you researched for the job position is a likely candidate for revenge."

"You're sure?"

"You can never be *sure* when human nature is involved, but I'd say there's very little probability."

"So that leaves the two divorce cases."

"There is one other avenue we haven't explored."

Lisa raised a questioning eyebrow.

"Old boyfriends. Did you break up with someone who didn't want to call it quits?"

"No."

Her tone let him know she considered this subject closed, but he found himself wanting to know if she had been involved with anyone since him. "How can you be so certain? I think it would be smart to check into this."

Lisa wished she had a name to give him, but... "I've been too busy taking care of Andy and earning a living to become romantically involved with anyone."

Deep within, Slade experienced pleasure. He'd been her first and now he knew that he'd been the only man she'd been with. With the pleasure was something that felt like a twinge of possessiveness. *Dangerous reactions,* he warned himself. They were too much like the ones he'd had toward Claudette. Determinedly, he disregarded them. "So what about someone you didn't date but who wanted to date you...someone who might not have taken rejection well?"

"I suppose I should be flattered that you think I could evoke such a strong reaction in a man." Lisa stopped herself. She was letting her bitterness that he didn't love her show. She schooled a nonchalance into her manner and even managed a shrug. "However, you're barking up the wrong tree there."

As Slade nodded his acceptance of her assessment, she rose from the table. Catching a glimpse of herself in the mirror, she cringed. Her nap had left her hair in wild disarray. Wanting something other than her companion to think about, she found her brush and began working to tame it.

Watching her, Slade noted that in spite of her recent bout with death, she stood tall and straight. She was a strong, independent woman. Claudette hadn't been. Her feelings had been easily bruised and physically he'd seen her as delicate, even fragile. Guilt washed over him. He'd let Claudette down. Not wanting to think about that, he rose. "How about dinner and a movie? We managed to get out of Seattle without a tail. And I haven't seen anyone suspicious today. It should be safe."

Anything was better than being sequestered in this room with him until morning, Lisa decided and agreed.

They asked at the desk about restaurants and chose a highly recommended Italian place.

Sitting there eating in a quiet, discrete corner, chosen because it had a view of the door and a wall at their backs, Lisa was reminded of their first meal together.

They'd been working on a case and had chosen an out-of-the-way table with a clear view of the door and the wall to their backs. They had been there waiting for the drug dealer Marcos Lane to arrive. Lisa had had a close friend die on the orders of Lane, who had been singled out as the key target of the drug task force operation. In spite of the rage she'd felt toward Lane and the single-mindedness of her desire to see him behind bars, she had found her attention wavering to her companion.

Then, too, she'd known about his devotion to his departed wife. It had been common gossip. He had dated, but only with the stipulation that the woman understood he would never become emotionally involved. Lisa found herself wondering if maybe he'd simply come up with the perfect line. A great many women would see him as a challenge...one they couldn't resist. He was good-looking in a rugged sort of way, strongly built and had the most charming smile when he chose to use it.

However, she was not a game player when it came to men. Other women might see him as an irresistible challenge but she'd prided herself on being smarter than that. She'd worked with him for a couple of weeks by then and knew how stubborn, demanding and authoritative he could be. He was, in her book, nothing but trouble.

Her mind snapped back to the present. *And he still is,* she added, forcing her attention back to the menu.

Slade, too, had been recalling the first time they'd eaten together. He'd known she didn't like him. He'd gone out of his way to make her angry with him. He'd wanted her to resign from the task force. From the moment she'd walked through the door of the drug task force briefing room, she'd made him uneasy. Her air of confidence irritated him. Confident rookies had a way of getting themselves killed. He'd double checked her credentials. There had been nothing there he could use to have her removed. She'd been second in her class and an expert marksman.

But twice he'd had a nightmare about her getting shot and woken in a cold sweat. He'd never had nightmares about any of his men before. He'd told himself it was because she was a woman and his chauvinist side was showing.

Slade took a terse breath. He should have kept his distance. His instincts had warned him she could be dangerous. Then he thought of Andy and his heart swelled with pride. Whether she liked it or not, he would always look after his child and Lisa, and he would find a way to be a part of their lives...a significant, daily part of their lives.

"Have you decided on what you would like?" the waiter asked, breaking into his thoughts.

Slade jerked his mind back to the menu and ordered.

Much later that night Lisa lay in her bed staring at the ceiling of the darkened room. She didn't want to, but she couldn't stop herself from remembering their first embrace. It had been a scene right out of the movies or one of those detective shows on television…the stereotypical embrace to keep from being noticed by the bad guys. But it had felt anything but stereotypical.

The fear had been real. Lane, a sociopath who killed at the drop of a hat, had surrounded himself with men who would do the same. When he'd left the restaurant, he'd chosen to walk. She and Slade were following at a discrete distance. The restaurant, a family owned and run place, was on the outskirts of Lubbock in the midst of a short block of stores in a blue collar residential area. Reaching a corner a couple blocks from the restaurant, they turned in the direction Lane had gone.

"He's made us," Slade murmured in her ear, the mike in his lapel picking up the warning, as well, and carrying it to their backup team.

Ahead of them, Lisa saw Lane leaning against the trunk of one of the trees lining the quiet road.

"Laugh like you're enjoying my nuzzling your neck," Slade ordered her, slowing their pace.

Lisa managed a giggle.

Slade pulled her into his arms, lifting her slightly so that he could shift their position to give her a view of the street behind them. "See anything?"

She'd known from the beginning that he considered her more of a liability than an asset. Because of that, she'd found it difficult to even be civil to him. But in spite of the tension between them, his nearness was causing her blood to rush and her legs to feel weak. Then she saw a sight that stiffened her with fear. "Two of his goons are coming up on us."

"Pretend you're upset by my advances. Push me away and stalk off across the street and head south. Take the first turn east."

Pretending she was upset was easy. She was—she couldn't believe how much she liked being in his arms. "Stop it!" she ordered. "I'm not that kind of girl." Breaking free, she strode across the street. Behind her, she could hear Slade cursing about women who tease and don't come through. Reaching the other side of the street, she glanced back to see him striding in the direction they'd come. Her breath locked in her lungs as he neared the goons.

Slowing her pace but forcing herself to keep moving in the direction he'd ordered, she reached into her purse to close her hand around the gun inside while watching Slade's progress out of the corner of her eye. If it looked as if he was in trouble, she was ready to come to his aid. But to her relief, the goons allowed him to pass without incident. Finally taking a breath, she hurried to the corner and turned left. Immediately hiding herself behind a trunk of a tree, she watched until Slade reached the corner in safety, crossed the street and headed down the main drag away from the restaurant. Only then did she ease out of her hiding place and, breaking into a jog, round the block.

Seeing Slade coming toward her, the remembered warmth of his embrace came back so strongly she could almost feel his arms around her. She'd known he was strong, but she'd never dreamed he could feel so sturdy. The way her body was reacting stunned her. Heat surged through her, igniting a fire deep within.

"You should have been here by the time I crossed the street," he snapped angrily. "When I tell you to take off, do it and don't dawdle."

His manner again reminded her that he considered her

more of a liability than an asset. The flames died a quick death. "I'm your partner. I wasn't going to simply desert you."

"I can take care of myself. What I don't need is to be worrying about you."

"You're not invincible, Slade Logan," she returned.

Catching her by the arm, he guided her toward the car. "You're my responsibility and I'm not letting anything happen to you."

Jerking free, she glared at him. "We're each other's responsibility. If I was a man, we wouldn't be having this discussion."

He frowned down at her. "You're right. We wouldn't." He continued toward the car. "We're calling it a night. I had Carl call in a second backup. He and Paul will be the primaries for the rest of the night."

Startled by his admission that if she had been a man he would be treating her differently, she accompanied him in silence. Once inside the car, she said in a more level voice, "That's a very chauvinistic attitude."

"I was brought up to protect the members of the female sex. It's ingrained in me. It's the way I am."

Lisa forced her mind back to the present, but the words *It's the way I am* continued to echo in her head. She should have taken those words to heart, but she hadn't. She'd thought she could change him. *Foolish, foolish girl.* Closing her eyes, she finally drifted into a restless sleep.

How to validate your
Editor's FREE GIFT "Thank You"

1. Peel off gift seal from front cover. Place it in space provided at right. This automatically entitles you to receive 2 FREE BOOKS and a fabulous mystery gift.

2. Send back this card and you'll get 2 brand-new Silhouette Romance® novels. These books have a cover price of $3.50 each in the U.S. and $3.99 each in Canada, but they are yours to keep absolutely free.

3. There's no catch. You're under no obligation to buy anything. We charge nothing—ZERO—for your first shipment. And you don't have to make any minimum number of purchases—not even one!

4. The fact is, thousands of readers enjoy receiving their books by mail from the Silhouette Reader Service™. They enjoy the convenience of home delivery...they like getting the best new novels at discount prices BEFORE they're available in stores...and they love their *Heart to Heart* subscriber newsletter featuring author news, horoscopes, recipes, book reviews and much more!

5. We hope that after receiving your free books you'll want to remain a subscriber. But the choice is yours— to continue or cancel, any time at all! So why not take us up on our invitation, with no risk of any kind. You'll be glad you did!

6. Don't forget to detach your FREE BOOKMARK. And remember...just for validating your Editor's Free Gift Offer, we'll send you THREE gifts, *ABSOLUTELY FREE!*

GET A FREE MYSTERY GIFT...

The Editor's "Thank You" Free Gifts Include:

- **Two BRAND-NEW romance novels!**
- **An exciting mystery gift!**

PLACE
FREE GIFT
SEAL
HERE

YES! I have placed my Editor's "Thank You" seal in the space provided above. Please send me 2 free books and a fabulous mystery gift. I understand I am under no obligation to purchase any books, as explained on the back and on the opposite page.

315 SDL DCQD

215 SDL DCP7
(S-R-OS-04/01)

NAME	(PLEASE PRINT CLEARLY)

ADDRESS

APT.#	CITY

STATE / PROV.	ZIP/POSTAL CODE

Thank You!

The Silhouette Reader Service™ — Here's how it works:

Accepting your 2 free books and gift places you under no obligation to buy anything. You may keep the books and gift and return the shipping statement marked "cancel." If you do not cancel, about a month later we'll send you 6 additional novels and bill you just $2.90 each in the U.S., or $3.25 each in Canada, plus 25¢ shipping & handling per book and applicable taxes if any.* That's the complete price and — compared to cover prices of $3.50 each in the U.S. and $3.99 each in Canada — it's quite a bargain! You may cancel at any time, but if you choose to continue, every month we'll send you 6 more books, which you may either purchase at the discount price or return to us and cancel your subscription.

*Terms and prices subject to change without notice. Sales tax applicable in N.Y. Canadian residents will be charged applicable provincial taxes and GST.

Chapter Seven

It was a little after noon when they arrived back in Seattle.

In the parking garage, Lisa fought to keep her mind focused on the people loading and unloading their cars. She'd dreamed about Slade during the night and was forced to admit that the physical attraction she'd felt for him in the past was as strong as ever. Reaching her mother's car, he ordered her to squat down out of view while he opened the door. Reluctantly obeying, her gaze was caught by his boots then began traveling up the sturdy columns of his jeans-clad legs. Fires of passion flamed to life. Furious with herself, she jerked her gaze to the concrete floor of the parking lot.

Once seated inside the car, something nagged at her...something she'd noticed on the floor just under her door. As Slade slid into the driver's seat, she suddenly realized what it was.

"Stop!" Lisa grabbed his wrist before he could put the key in the ignition. "I saw a thin piece of wire under

my door.'' She paused then added, ''It was the kind of
wire used in the car bombing we were sure Lane had
ordered.''

''If you're right, there's no telling what will trigger it.
Just sit still and call the police,'' Slade ordered.

Lisa hesitated. ''If I'm wrong we're going to look really stupid.''

''Better safe than sorry,'' he returned.

Taking her cell phone out of her purse, she dialed
9-1-1.

The bomb squad responded immediately and it didn't
take them long to find the explosive. It was under the
hood, wired to blow when the ignition was turned on.

''Amateurish but effective,'' the captain of the bomb
squad told them as his men removed it. ''The kind of
thing a person can find out how to construct on the Internet these days.''

Detective Overson arrived on the scene at that moment. ''Looks like someone is after you,'' he said as the
bomb was put into a container and taken away.

''I'd say that's pretty evident,'' Lisa returned dryly.

Overson gave her an indulgent look. ''I still think
Tommy Cross was the intended victim when you were
shot. Whoever fired at him was a pro. This bomb was
amateurish and so was the hit-and-run. Whoever is after
you is no pro. With any luck we'll be able to track down
the components of the bomb and get a description of the
buyer.'' His tone became authoritative. ''I think it's time
you turned those files over to me.''

With her life on the line, Lisa decided she'd rather stay
in charge. ''Not yet.''

Overson scowled. ''I don't like this. That bomb was
no joke.'' He turned to Slade. ''It could have taken out
both of you.''

Slade's gaze leveled on Lisa. Whomever this killer was, he was getting more and more dangerous. He wanted Lisa out of the line of fire. "He's right. Do you want Andy to be minus two parents?"

Tears of frustration brimmed in her eyes. "I can't go near my child until this lunatic is caught." Her gaze turned to Detective Overson. "If I give you the files we have left, when will you get to them?"

"I have to be in court all day tomorrow and maybe early next week, but I'll start looking into your case as soon as I'm finished testifying," he promised.

"What about another detective looking into it sooner?" Slade asked.

"Everyone is doing double and triple duty. Take Miss Gray someplace safe. I promise you, I'll devote my full time to her case as soon as I'm free."

Lisa's jaw hardened. "You give me a call when you have the time to start. If I haven't found out who's after me by then, I'll consider handing over the files to you."

"You do what you can with the bomb components," Slade said. "I'll watch over her."

One of the bomb squad members approached them. "Your car's safe to drive now," he informed Slade, then walked away.

Overson's gaze traveled over the two of them. "I don't want to see anything happen to either of you. If you weren't trained lawmen, I'd consider locking you up for your own good for withholding evidence. But that wouldn't serve any purpose. Besides, a judge probably wouldn't allow it."

Driving away, Slade glared at the road ahead. "We're going to follow one of Overson's suggestions. I'm taking you someplace safe and you're going to stay there until I find out who's after you.''

The thought that Slade could be killed because of her had shaken her to the core. ''You're going home and looking after our son. I'm going to finish this myself,'' she returned curtly.

''You can't really believe I would do that?''

''That's the way I want it. Like you said, it wouldn't be fair to Andy to lose both parents. If you stay with me, that could happen.''

''If I leave and you get yourself killed, I could never face him,'' Slade countered. He gave her hand a squeeze. ''We'll find your would-be killer and end it.''

His touch didn't warm her. It only served to increase the fear building within. ''I don't want Andy to be left an orphan. I never dreamed that first shot was for me.''

Slade heard the guilt in her voice. ''I suppose if you had known, you'd have insisted on handling it on your own...just left a letter telling me about Andy in the event anything went wrong.'' His voice took on a harsh edge. ''That would have left a hell of a lot of loose ends for me to clean up.''

''That would have been better than this. I came to you because I was worried about Andy being parentless. Now I've put us both in harm's way.''

''I'd have come up here and hunted your killer down on my own. At least this way we have each other to guard our respective backsides.''

Lisa had to admit he had a point, but she still didn't like it. She also knew further arguing with him would be futile. She was equally convinced that if she turned this matter over to the police, they might never find the person. Or if they did, it could take months. With grim reluctance, she gave a shrug of concession.

"Our first stop is going to be the local FBI office," Slade said. "I called a friend in the Bureau while the bomb squad was doing their job. The local branch is going to loan us a bug detector. Could be whoever is after you put monitoring devices on all the cars at your place. That would explain how they located this car. And if they did, they hid it well. I gave this car a once-over after the bomb was removed and couldn't find anything."

A short time later, they pulled into a midtown garage where they were met by Agent Stevens. A search of the car found no bug.

"Most likely, you did have a bug on you and the killer removed it when he planted the bomb," Stevens said. "They're expensive little gadgets. He wouldn't have wanted to blow it up." He nodded toward the device in Slade's hand. "Check the car every time it's been out of your sight."

They thanked him and left.

Making certain they weren't being followed, Slade found a motel on the outskirts of town. They got dinner from a fast food restaurant and took it to their room.

While they ate, Lisa glanced at the remaining two files, discarded one and picked up the other. "Randolph Granger must have found out I was the one who uncovered that hidden bank account and those property deeds. It cost him a quarter of a million more in the divorce settlement."

Slade glanced through the other file. An expression of disbelief came over his face. "This Milton Blout hired you to find out if his wife was abusing their dog so he could win the custody battle for the animal?"

Lisa gave him a dry look. "Some people are as attached to their pets as others are to their children." She shrugged. ''But I don't know why I even pulled that file. Once I'd satisfied my client that his wife was a responsible person, he was happy. The truth is, I think he really wanted to find out if she had a boyfriend. She didn't. It's just that I thought I should pull everything I'd worked on for the past six months.''

Slade put the Blout file aside and placed a call to Boyd. Hanging up, he said, ''Every felon you helped send to jail has been accounted for. None could have carried out the attacks on you.''

''The list of possible suspects is getting shorter by the minute,'' Lisa muttered. Picking up the phone, she dialed Beth Granger's number. There was no answer and she didn't want to leave a message on the answering machine that might lead the killer to her. Hanging up, she yawned widely. ''We'll contact her tomorrow. I'm too tired to deal with anything more tonight.''

Finishing her meal, she stretched out on the bed. ''You can take the first shower.''

As soon as the bathroom door was closed, she shoved the Granger file inside her suitcase, then waited until she heard the water running. Satisfied Slade was in the shower, she headed to the door. Her hand was on the knob when he stepped out of the bathroom, still dressed, and pressed a hand on the door to prevent her from opening it. ''Figured you were getting ready to run,'' he said with a disapproving scowl.

''I won't make you a target. For Andy's sake, you've got to let me see this through on my own,'' she pleaded.

''For Andy's sake I'm going to see we both make it through this.'' He regarded her impatiently. ''Besides, what good would running now do? I've got those files memorized. I'd be bird-dogging your tail by morning.''

"Bird-dogging is preferable to being a sitting duck at my side," she returned.

"Like I said earlier, bird-dogging would mean I'd have to be keeping an eye on my backside as well as yours. Your would-be killer has to know I've been helping you. Together we can watch out for each other." A determined expression came over his face. "Besides, have you forgotten that tomorrow is our wedding day?" Abruptly a grim expression spread over his face. "Or maybe that was why you were running?"

Finding the bomb had put everything but worrying about his safety out of her mind. "I had forgotten," she said stiffly.

It irked him that she found their nuptials so minor.

Seeing the flash of anger on his face, she gave him a dry look. "Well, it's not as if you really want to marry *me*."

"I will not allow my son to grow up with the label of bastard."

Lisa realized she'd been hoping that he'd say he wasn't marrying her just for their son's sake. *Foolish, stupid girl.*

"Am I going to have to handcuff you to something in this room or are you going to behave?" he asked threateningly.

Grudgingly admitting to herself that she couldn't change the course of her investigation, she issued a disgruntled sigh and strode back to her bed. While Slade returned to the bathroom, this time to really shower, Lisa lay glaring at the ceiling, silently cursing his thickheadedness. But in the midst of her anger, the sound of the running water brought back old memories...memories of a time when she would have climbed in with him. Sucking in a shaky breath, her mind wandered again to their first kiss. A bittersweet smile curled the corners of her

mouth. That had been a shock to both of them. After the
short embrace they'd shared while tailing Lane, Slade
had been even cooler toward her. She'd been certain he
didn't like her. And she'd told herself she was glad. The
last thing she had wanted was to get involved with a man
who was totally devoted to his dead wife.

She then remembered the night they went to arrest
Lane, who preferred death to prison. There had been a
shootout and he'd gotten away. Lisa had been in the middle of the firefight. Afterward, Slade had gotten her alone
and read her the riot act for placing herself in the line of
fire.

She'd been furious with him and pointed out that she'd
only been doing her job and that it was his chauvinistic
side overreacting because she was a woman.

"So maybe I am too much of a chauvinist," he'd conceded.

She'd been stunned by his admission. But even more
shocked by the gruff emotion in his voice.

Then he'd added, "But I don't want to see you get
hurt."

She'd been meeting his gaze with defiant pride. Suddenly the defiance was gone and her knees were weak-
ening. The hard hickory-brown of his eyes had softened
and she was being drawn into warm dark depths she'd
never believed existed within him. The heat had inten-
sified until she could barely breathe. He'd taken a step
toward her, then she was in his arms and their lips had
met.

Even now, years later, passion still flared to life at the
memory.

The bittersweet smile on her face became more pro-
nounced. They'd both been stunned. For a long moment
they'd just stood looking at each other, then Slade had

walked off without a word. *Too bad I didn't leave it at that,* she mused. In the next instant she thought of Andy. He was worth the price she'd paid.

When Slade came back into the room, she went in to take her shower. Standing there with the water cascading over her, she recalled their second kiss. She'd instigated it.

Because Lane was still on the loose, they had been forced to continue working together. But Slade had been keeping his distance as much as possible and had become even more frosty toward her.

For a week she'd battled in her mind. She'd never had that intense a reaction to a kiss. And then there was the heat she'd seen in his eyes. It had been so intense, just thinking about it had taken her breath away.

A part of her had argued that his coldness was because he truly regretted his momentary lapse and felt nothing for her, while another part argued that she'd cracked the barrier he kept around his heart and he was afraid any further contact with her might destroy it. In the end, the hope that it was the latter prevailed.

She'd started flirting with him, very subtly, but flirting nonetheless. He'd ignored it. She'd tried convincing herself that he really didn't care and it would be best for her to forget him. But just seeing him had caused her juices to flow. Finally it had been anger toward herself that had made her insist on the kiss. She'd tried reasoning with herself, pointing out that he'd obviously had no feelings for her and it was foolish of her to be nursing this infatuation. But reason had refused to prevail. It had gotten to the point that when he'd walk into a room, fire would spread through her. When their bodies brushed, currents of heated electricity flowed from the contact.

Unable to stand it any longer, she'd decided to end the

irrational behavior once and for all. She'd been certain that a second kiss was the solution. The first had been unexpected. That had made it exciting...an adventure. The second would be planned...mundane...and it would end the silly infatuation.

It was a Thursday evening. She'd chosen not to call to tell him she was coming over to his place. The notion that he might have a date and seeing him with someone else had become part of her hope for a cure. Or maybe he'd be such a slob it would be an immediate turn-off and she wouldn't even have to kiss him again. But no one had been there except him and his place had felt comfortable...definitely masculine, but comfortable.

He hadn't been pleased to see her.

"Do you mind asking me inside?" she'd prompted when he continued to remain blocking his doorway.

He'd stepped aside, giving her plenty of room to pass him without contact. "So why are you here?"

"It's an experiment. No, that's not quite right. It's more of an exorcism."

He'd raised an eyebrow at that statement.

Embarrassment had threatened to stop her, but she'd come that far and would not turn back. "It's that kiss."

Slade had said nothing. He'd simply continued to regard her with cold control.

"I know this sounds schoolgirlish, but I can't get it out of my mind. I want to kiss you a second time."

"I don't think that's such a good idea."

His standoffishness should have been enough to stop her, but it hadn't been. Her need to know how his lips would feel the second time was too strong. Silently she'd cursed herself. "I know you aren't interested in doing this, but this isn't for you, it's for me. I just want you out of my system."

Slade had backed farther away. "I don't want any kind of personal relationship."

"I don't, either. At least, not with you. I know all about your devotion to your first wife. Do you think I like finding you in my dreams? Being distracted by you on the job? You're not even close to the kind of man I would consider marrying. I want someone who's sensitive, gentle, caring. You're just a big brute of a man. Oh, you have good enough manners and you're polite. But you're also a stone wall. I just want to get this over and done with and get on with my life."

Slade had continued to stand stiffly rigid, matching her description of a stone wall perfectly.

Approaching him, she'd placed a hand on each shoulder and had to go up on her tiptoes to reach his mouth. She'd expected his lips to feel cold. Instead they'd been warm. And she'd planned to keep the contact short, just a peck. Instead, once her mouth found his, it had wanted to stay and enjoy the taste.

Then Slade's arms had wound around her and he'd added his energy to the kiss.

The rest was a delicious, erotic blur that had amazed both of them. Neither had even considered hesitating. It was as if their bodies belonged together and reason, thought—everything but their physical need for each other—was blocked out.

Afterward, Slade had been uncomfortable. Too late he'd realized she was still a virgin. He'd apologized for taking that from her.

She'd told him she had wanted him as much as he'd wanted her and that what had happened was even more her fault than his. After all, she had been the one to come to him. Down deep inside, she'd wanted to be angry with herself for having given in to passion and not waiting until her wedding night, but it had felt so right.

Slade had been blatantly blunt about their having no future together. His heart, he'd said, belonged to Claudette and always would.

She recalled how her pride had kicked in and she could still hear herself saying that it wasn't his heart that had interested her. She'd left in the middle of the night, planning to never repeat that mistake. The problem was, it hadn't really felt like a mistake. Her rational, reasonable side, knew it was. But her body... She took a long, shaky breath. Her body craved his.

Still, she'd made herself act as if nothing had happened between them. He had been clearly relieved by this and life went on as it had before. Then he'd gotten the flu, a really bad one that had lasted a couple of weeks. She hadn't been able to stay away. She'd gone to his place and insisted on staying with him until he was cured. He'd been brusque with her, keeping her at a distance, treating her like an interloper. But she hadn't been able to make herself leave. She'd known he was worried she wanted an emotional involvement. She'd told him point-blank that he was safe from her. Still, he had continued to accept her presence grudgingly.

On top of that, for her trouble, she'd gotten sick. Her mother had moved to Seattle and she'd been on her own. To her surprise, Slade had shown up on her doorstep and insisted on taking care of her. And he had done a surprisingly tender job of it.

Lisa closed her eyes and groaned. It had been that tenderness that had encouraged her to believe he could learn to care for her. She'd pursued an affair with him and, assured by her that she understood the boundaries, he'd been a willing participant.

"The problem was, I wasn't being honest with him. I was sure I could break down those boundaries," she grumbled to herself as she turned off the water, then dried herself and went to bed.

She had learned a very valuable lesson she would not forget.

Chapter Eight

Lisa groaned in protest when she felt herself being shaken awake.

"Time to get up. We've got an appointment to get married today."

She opened one eye to see Slade looking down at her with an impatient expression and she forced herself out of bed. *No romantic fairy-tale wedding for me,* she mused dryly. *More like a blip on the radar screen of my life.*

A short while later they were pulling into a fast-food place for breakfast. Lisa glanced at her watch. "I can't believe you got a judge to get up this early."

"We're heading up the coast. I want to get married without having to worry about someone trying to kill you halfway through the ceremony," he said. "I've checked for bugs. And, once we're outside of town, no one will be able to tail us without us noticing."

He sounded and looked like a man on his way to perform a particularly grim duty. Her shoulders squared with pride. "You're obviously not happy about going through with this marriage, so let's call it off. I told you it wasn't necessary.''

''We're going through with the marriage.''

''I'm not repeating vows with a man who would obviously prefer to be hanging over a fiery pit.''

''A fiery pit would be easier to deal with than me keeping my hands off of you.''

Lisa was stunned into silence. He'd been behaving as if he was having no trouble at all. ''Really?''

He glanced at her, then returned his attention to the road. ''It's been a long time since I've been with a woman.''

Lisa was certain she caught an edge of uneasiness in his voice and a thought struck her. ''How long?''

Slade shrugged. ''A long time.''

He was hedging. She'd never known Slade to hedge. ''Are you saying you haven't been with a woman since me?'' The minute she asked the question, she wished she hadn't. He was probably trying not to tell her that he'd had several female friends since she left.

''Decided I should concentrate on my job.''

Lisa sat back and smiled to herself. *Don't go thinking that this means something important,* her inner voice insisted on cautioning. *You're only going to get hurt again.* The smile faded.

Angry with herself for being tempted to go down a road she knew would only cause her pain, Lisa concentrated on trying to spot a tail. There was practically no traffic and when they left the main road, no one turned off after them. By the time Slade pulled into the parking area beside a small chapel, they were both certain they had arrived alone.

Lisa's gaze traveled over the small, white-shingled, steepled building. *Now this could have come out of a fairy tale,* she thought. The chapel and its setting were charming. An oval garden surrounded an ornately carved wooden sign informing her that this was the Woodland Wedding Chapel. Lisa had heard about this place. It was considered one of the more romantic places to get married. She'd also heard that it was normally booked solid for months, even years, in advance. "I hope you made an appointment."

"Everything has been taken care of."

She continued to eye him with surprise. This was definitely not something she'd expected. "How in the world did you find out about this place?"

"I asked the manager at the hotel we stayed at after we got Andy, your mother and your aunt on the plane. I figured since we wouldn't have the time to dress for the event, I should find a nice setting for the wedding."

Lisa glanced down at the lightweight sweater, chino slacks and sneakers she was wearing. Slade wasn't wearing anything fancier—jeans, a blue, button-down shirt and cowboy boots. And, then there was his badge and the leather holster housing his weapon. She wondered if he was going to take them off. He didn't.

Entering the chapel, a man dressed in a black suit, white shirt and black tie started toward them from the front of the aisle. Midway into his first stride, he suddenly went into slow motion, then stopped abruptly.

Lisa saw the man's gaze fix on Slade's gun and the color drain from his face. Then his gaze shifted slightly and the color returned. He'd obviously seen Slade's badge. "Is there a problem, Officer?" he asked, regaining mobility and continuing toward them.

"No problem," Slade replied.

The man squinted at Slade's badge as he came nearer.

"You're a Texas Ranger. Aren't you a little far from home?"

"I'm Slade Logan. I assume you're Reverend Johnson?" Slade extended his hand toward the man. "I called and arranged for you to marry us."

The man looked them up and down. "When you said you wanted a nice but quick ceremony and wouldn't take up much of my time, I guess you meant it." He glanced at his watch. "We'd better get started. I've got a large wedding scheduled in two hours. The bride's mother has been a basket case and I expect her to show up at any moment to make certain everything is just the way she ordered." His gaze went back to Slade's gun. "And I'd appreciate it if you'd leave that outside."

"Someone has tried three times to kill my fiancée. I was careful to make sure we weren't followed but I think I'll just keep my gun with me." Slade's refusal was polite but firm.

Lisa noticed that the Reverend Johnson suddenly looked very uncomfortable again.

"Well. Yes. Right," the man stammered. He motioned for them to go in opposite directions. "We'll just take our places. Lisa..." He paused to look at Slade. "I believe you said your fiancée's name was Lisa Gray."

"Right," Slade replied.

The reverend returned his attention to Lisa. "You stand at the end of the aisle." He turned back to Slade. "You come with me to the front."

"You said you would provide music," Slade reminded him.

The reverend bobbed his head. "I'll be right back." Moving swiftly for a man his age, he hurried down the aisle and exited through a door at the rear of the chapel.

"Maybe you shouldn't have mentioned that someone

is trying to kill me," Lisa said. "I think that unnerved him."

"Sure got him moving fast," Slade noted as the man returned with an elderly man in tow.

"This is my organist, Paul Hansen." Reverend Johnson made quick introductions.

Lisa noted that Paul Hansen looked as if he would have preferred to be someplace else.

"Paul, you take your place and as soon as Lisa and Slade are in position, you may begin."

"Flowers?" Slade said in a reminding tone.

"Yes. Yes, flowers." The reverend again jogged back through the door at the rear of the chapel. He returned momentarily with a lovely bouquet of roses and handed it to Lisa. "Now you wait at the far end of the aisle until the music begins, then come down the aisle to us," he instructed over his shoulder, motioning Slade to accompany him to the altar.

As soon as they were all in place, the reverend gave the organist the nod to begin the music. Lisa thought that he was playing the tune a bit on the fast side, then her gaze focused on Slade and everything else vanished from her mind. He looked so handsome and he was waiting to marry her. In her dreams this moment had happened. However, there he'd been marrying her because he was in love with her. *But he isn't and never will be,* she told herself sternly. Even this dose of reality couldn't stop the nervous excitement that bubbled inside her as she reached him and the reverend began leading them through their wedding vows.

For a moment Lisa was amused by how quickly the reverend was going through the ceremony, then she remembered that the rite traditionally ended with a kiss. Suddenly all she could think about was whether or not

Slade would follow this tradition. His admission of how hard it was for him to keep his hands off of her played through her mind. Then the moment was there.

"I think we'll keep that kiss for later," Slade said stiffly. "Best get the license signed and be on our way."

Lisa was certain they hadn't been followed and there was no need to rush. She was also certain she caught a flash of fear in Slade's eyes. Was he that afraid she might break down the barrier he kept around his heart? *More likely, he's worried that if he kisses me, lust will take hold of both of us, we'll be intimate again and I'll start thinking just what I'm thinking now and he doesn't want to lead me on.*

The reverend was happy to comply with shortening the ceremony in any way. Within minutes the legal formalities were completed and Lisa and Slade were back in her mother's car. As Slade began to back out, Lisa glanced down at her ringless finger. They'd gone through the motions, but she didn't feel married. *Because marriages are supposed to at least start with the assumption they're going to last. And this one hasn't got a chance.* She knew her limitations. She couldn't live out her life being just a warm body that filled a physical void in Slade's life. She wanted a husband who loved her.

Her gaze shifted to the view through the front windshield. Something wasn't right. "Were you running the air conditioner on the way here?" She didn't think he had been, but then she'd been much more tense about this wedding than she'd wanted to admit.

Slade had been concentrating on what was behind them. Looking to the front, he frowned and braked. "No."

"Wrong color, anyway," Lisa muttered, her gaze

locked on the pool of liquid that had been under the front end of the car.

"Get down," Slade ordered, turning off the car and climbing out. It only took him a moment to check the puddle. Returning, he got out a flashlight and made a quick inspection of the underside of the car. "The brake line's been cut."

Lisa eased up out of her seat just enough to look around. "But how did whoever wants me dead find us here?"

Slade shook his head. "I don't know. The car wasn't bugged and I know we weren't followed." He rounded the car to her door. "Come on. I'm taking you back inside until we can get a tow truck for your mother's car and a ride back to Seattle for us."

The reverend and the organist were not happy to see Lisa and Slade returning to the chapel. "We need a tow service," Slade said.

"That would be Jake Reynolds," Reverend Johnson said. He turned on his heels and headed at a near trot to the back of the sanctuary, adding over his shoulder, "I'll call him."

Lisa noted that the organist quickly scurried back to his seat at the organ, clearly wanting to put distance between himself and them.

Returning a couple of minutes later, the reverend informed them that the tow truck was on its way.

"I'd like a word with you and your organist and anyone else who's here," Slade said, his tone making this an order.

"We're the only ones here," Reverend Johnson replied, motioning for Paul Hansen to join them.

Slade faced the two men grimly. "Our brake line was cut."

"Are you saying the man who's trying to kill your wife is here?" Paul Hansen asked, his complexion pale.

"Yes, and I'd like to know how he found out we were going to be here." Slade's gaze raked over the two of them. "I didn't tell anyone. I didn't even tell Lisa."

"Well, we certainly didn't tell anyone," Reverend Johnson returned. "You must have been followed."

"We weren't followed."

"Maybe there's one of those tailing devices on your car," the organist suggested.

"Checked it first thing this morning," Slade returned.

Lisa noticed the reverend shift uneasily. "Do you know something we should know?"

"Someone did call a couple of days ago. A man." The reverend paused, then said, "At least, I think it was. Actually, I can't be certain. Whoever it was spoke in a gruff voice…said they had a bad cold. The person claimed to be a friend of yours and said you'd asked him or her to check on the arrangements…make certain everything was as agreed upon."

"I didn't ask anyone to call you."

The reverend regarded Slade with defiance. "You also didn't mention that someone was trying to kill your bride."

Lisa continued to regard the men with a frown of confusion. "But how did he or she know to call here?"

Silence followed her question.

Suddenly the front door of the chapel burst open.

Slade spun around, his gun out of its holster before the turn was complete.

"There's a car just sitting in the middl—" The shrill complaint of the woman who had just entered stopped in midword, her gaze locked on the gun being pointed at her.

"Mrs. Varney." Realizing she was in danger of fainting, the reverend rushed to her side.

"Sorry, ma'am," Slade apologized, reholstering the gun.

"What's going on here?" the woman gasped.

"Nothing you need concern yourself with," the reverend assured her, taking her arm to steady her.

She wasn't listening. Her gaze had gone from Slade's gun to his badge. "It's my daughter's fiancé, isn't it? He's wanted by the law. I knew it. I knew it."

"What's going on?" a male voice demanded.

Looking past the woman at the door, Lisa saw a man who appeared to be in his late twenties, dressed in a tuxedo, entering with three other men in tuxedos.

"Your past has caught up with you and not a minute too soon," Mrs. Varney announced with self-righteous indignation.

"What the devil are you talking about?" the oldest of the group of men demanded.

Mrs. Varney motioned toward Slade. "The law is here to arrest your son."

"Arrest me for what?" The first young man glowered at Slade.

"We're just waiting for a tow truck," Slade said in an easy drawl.

The woman spun around, glaring at him. "You pulled a gun on me."

"So you don't think my son is good enough for your daughter." The older man strode toward the woman. "Well, I'll tell you what I think. I like Janet just fine, but I've told him that getting you for a mother-in-law might not be worth it. You're a nosey, irritating, busybody."

Past the group at the door, Slade saw the tow truck

arrive. "Stay out of the line of fire," he whispered in Lisa's ear, and headed out to meet the driver.

Lisa had the feeling he wasn't just talking about her would-be killer. Taking a position just inside the door, she felt sorry for the bride who would be showing up to discover her wedding was in danger of becoming a brawl.

By the time the tow truck driver had their car hooked up, the groom, his father and his groomsmen had stalked off to a room at the rear of the chapel, leaving Mrs. Varney glaring at their backs and the reverend looking like a man who wished he'd stayed in bed for the day.

Seeing Slade give her a wave to join him, she hurried out to the tow truck and climbed into the middle of the seat.

"Jake is going to give us a tow to his garage," Slade said. "He's right next door to the police station. We'll have them bag the cut line and anything else that looks like it might be useful in our investigation. Then Jake will check the car thoroughly for any evidence of further tampering and install a new line while we wait in the police station."

Lisa thanked the man.

"You're lucky whoever cut your line wasn't smart enough to only cut it a little so the fluid would drain slowly. If you'd gotten out on Old Ridge Road with no brakes, you could've gone over the cliff and into the ravine."

A chill swept through Lisa and she turned to Slade. "You've got to let me handle this on my own."

"No way," he returned.

Jake nodded his agreement. "A man's got to protect his woman."

"Men," Lisa muttered.

* * *

A couple of hours later they were on their way back to Seattle, the cut hose bagged in the back seat, to be turned over to Detective Overson.

"Definitely a wedding day I won't soon forget," Lisa said, using the side mirror to watch the traffic behind them.

"Any sign we're being followed?" Slade asked.

"None."

"I suppose whoever is after you could have followed us to the hotel the night I made the call to the chapel, but they couldn't possibly have tapped into the line and the call wasn't listed on the bill because I used my calling card. So how did they know where the ceremony was going to take place?"

Lisa recalled a recent movie she'd seen. "I know there's supposed to be safeguards, but there could be a chance a really good hacker could have gotten into your calling card records."

Slade frowned. "Maybe. Or, he could have found a way to get into my credit card account. I used it to pay the reverend. Like you said, those accounts are supposed to be protected, but we can't overlook those possibilities, especially since they seem to be the only ones we can come up with." He glanced toward her. "So are any of the people in those last two files hackers?"

"Not that I'm aware of." Lisa groaned in frustration. "I purposely took cases that weren't dangerous. I'll admit serving papers on Tommy Cross was a little iffy, but it was out in broad daylight and I was just serving him with a subpoena."

"Overson could be right about you not being the target of that first shot. That did take a marksman and if it is the same person, you'd think they'd continue to use a gun. Instead, they've tried a new method each time."

Lisa picked up the Granger folder. "Time to give Beth Granger another call."

Again she got no answer.

"Until we reach her, we'll see what we can find out about Randolph Granger's movements on our own," Slade said.

Lisa frowned. "I've sort of lost track of the days. It's Saturday, right?"

"Right." Slade suddenly found himself recalling a long weekend they'd spent in Dallas when he'd lost track of the days. She'd had to remind him when the time came to go home. "I'd like to go back to the way things were," he said bluntly.

Confusion showed on Lisa's face. "The way things were?"

"With us," he elaborated, realizing he'd lost her with his quick change in subject.

She frowned at him. "We've been through this. I want more than just lust in a relationship."

"We had more than lust," he argued. "We were friends as well as lovers. The only difference now is that we're married."

Lisa told herself that being married didn't make his suggestion any more palatable. But deep inside was a weakness for him that was hard to fight. When he touched her, he made her feel alive in ways nothing else did. Just the thought of being with him caused her blood to race and her skin to flush. Even as she ordered herself to tell him no, she heard herself saying, "I'll think about it."

"I'd appreciate that." Stopping at a light, Slade turned to face her. "We could make a good family...you, me and Andy. I may not be your idea of a great father, but I can promise you, I'll do my best."

Lisa recalled the tenderness she'd seen in his eyes when he was around Andy. "Wanting to be a good father is an important first step."

A crooked, pleased smile tilted one corner of Slade's mouth as he returned his attention to the road. She hadn't refused his request, that meant there was a chance she would accept. And he wanted her to agree more than he'd wanted anything in a long time. This realization caused a wave of uneasiness. He didn't like caring so much. *It's my duty to provide a family environment for my son,* he told himself.

Lisa knew she'd be asking for trouble if she went along with Slade's request. Not wanting to think about it, she turned her mind back to their case. Punching in the number for information, she asked for Granger's number, then saying she wanted to be certain she had the right Randolph Granger, she asked for his address. "He should be home. He rarely went anywhere," she said, giving Slade directions to get them to his new residence.

On the way to Granger's place, Lisa again tried calling Beth. This time she got an answer.

"As much as I'd like to see Randolph behind bars, I doubt it's him," Beth said when Lisa finished explaining the reason for her call.

Lisa had never heard Beth sound so hostile. "Did something happen?"

"The creep. When we were married, he would never spend any money, never do anything. And he made me account for every cent I spent. As soon as the divorce went through, he became the world's biggest swinger. Took a trip to Europe. Went on a cruise. My only consolation is that he also went skiing and broke both legs. He's been in a hospital in Colorado in traction for the past four weeks."

"Oh," was all Lisa could think of to say.

"But don't get me wrong. I'm glad I divorced him. I've started a business with my sister and we're having a ball."

"That brings us back to square one once again," Lisa muttered unhappily as she pressed the end button.

"There's one file left," Slade reminded her.

"I can't believe anyone would want to kill me over a dog. Besides, like I said, they ended up with mutual custody. The wife got the pooch during the week and the husband got him on weekends. He even called me to thank me for doing such a thorough job and putting his mind at ease."

"Still, we might as well check him out." Slade glanced into the back seat. "But first we'll drop our evidence off at police headquarters."

Detective Overson, who was at the station reviewing his testimony for Monday, wasn't happy to learn of this latest attempt on Lisa's life. But he also agreed that turning over the files she'd already checked in to wouldn't do any good. And he agreed with her that the last file didn't look promising. "If I were you, I'd sit down and think long and hard about any enemies I might have made over the years," he suggested. "In the meantime, I'll have our forensic department take a look at the brake line. With any luck, they might find a fingerprint." Pointedly he added, "And when you have that list, you give it to me. If you won't go into hiding, at least we can both be working toward finding your would-be killer."

Thanking him for his help, Lisa and Slade left. Certain it was a waste of time, but not knowing what else to do, Lisa gave Slade directions to the apartment of Milton Blout.

No one answered the knock on the door.

"That place is vacant."

Lisa turned to see a young woman with a bag of groceries in her arms coming down the hall. "Milton Blout doesn't live here anymore?"

The woman shook her head. "He moved out a couple of months ago."

"Do you know where he went?" Slade asked.

The woman was eyeing Slade's badge and gun. "I find it hard to believe he could be in any trouble. He was such a mild-mannered man."

Slade smiled. "He isn't. We just need some information from him."

Lisa saw the woman's eyes sparkle. Slade could turn on the charm when he wanted to.

"He moved back home. He and his wife reconciled."

Thanking the woman for her help, they headed back to the car. "If what the neighbor said is true, that kills any motive Milton or his wife might have," Lisa stated.

"We should still talk to him."

"But not at his house. If he and his wife have reconciled, I don't want to show up on his doorstep and cause trouble. She might not like the idea that he had her investigated." Back in the car, Lisa opened the Blout file, found his home phone number and punched it in. She was relieved when Milton answered.

"My wife and I are just on our way out," he said when she asked if he could meet with her. "Come by tomorrow morning around ten for brunch."

"Your wife knows about me?"

"Yes. I thought she'd asked for the divorce because she had a boyfriend," Milton admitted.

Mentally, Lisa gave herself a point for being right.

"When you assured me that wasn't the case," he continued, "I decided I had a chance to win her back. I sent her flowers and asked her out on a date. She admitted that the only reason she'd wanted a divorce was because she felt neglected and I told her I had thought she'd had a boyfriend. After we reconciled, I told her about hiring you. She was flattered."

In the background, Lisa heard a woman asking who he was talking to. "Lisa Gray, the detective I hired when I thought you had a boyfriend."

The woman laughed and said, "I'm dying to meet her."

Milton returned his attention to Lisa. "You heard that. You have to come to brunch."

Clearly these two weren't suspect, Lisa concluded. "I appreciate the invitation, but I have some other business I need to take care of tomorrow," she said. Thanking him for the invitation and agreeing to get together with them sometime when she wasn't so busy, she rang off.

"Another dead end," she told Slade glumly.

"It's time to call it a day, anyway," he said, noting the tired lines beginning to form on her face. He frowned at the phone in her hand. "I've been thinking about your suggestion that your would-be killer is tracking us by tapping into our phone or credit card records. It's a possibility we can't ignore. Until we find out how he's finding us, I'll let the family know not to call us unless it's an emergency. We'll turn your phone off and keep mine on in case Detective Overson needs to contact us. Any calls we make, we'll make from pay phones. As for money, we'll use cash. And I'll get it from bank machines that are on our way to someplace else."

Lisa nodded her agreement.

Chapter Nine

A while later, Lisa lay in bed listening to the shower running and wondering what would happen next. During dinner, Slade had said nothing more about consummating their marriage. In fact, they'd barely talked at all. She'd been too tired to even try to make small talk and Slade had always been the silent type.

On the way back to the car, he'd put an arm around her waist for support and apologized for not making certain she got more rest. There had been a tenderness in his attentiveness that had made her want to snuggle closer to him, but pride had kept her from doing that. Still, the imprint of his touch lingered on her skin.

If Slade turned out to be as good a father as his first encounter with Andy would suggest, she told herself, for her son's sake, she should try to make this marriage work. Her inner voice mocked her. *Who are you kidding?* She was looking for an excuse to be with him again. And why shouldn't she? He'd never lied to her or been unkind. *But he doesn't love you and never will.*

Slade came out of the bathroom, a towel draped around his hips. Clearly he'd decided that there was no reason for any further modesty between them. On the other hand, he'd gotten a room with two double beds. Well, she certainly wasn't going to make the first move. That had been her original mistake. Once she'd had a taste of him, she'd become an instant addict.

Slade, apparently, didn't even debate with himself. He shed the towel, climbed into her bed and turned off the light.

Just the brief glimpse of him sparked a fire in Lisa. Still, she lay stiffly, determined to let him make the next move.

"I know you're tired, but I'm willing to do all the work to get this marriage consummated," Slade said huskily, turning toward her and caressing her cheek with his hand.

She'd always been amazed by how gentle he could be for a man with such a tough exterior. Lisa wanted to play hard to get, but she couldn't muster any resistance. "I suppose if you're willing to do all the work..." She left the sentence dangling.

Slade breathed an inner sigh of relief. He'd prepared himself to accept her refusal but it wouldn't have been easy. The physical attraction he'd felt for her in the past had been incredibly strong and had not faded during the time they were apart. It seemed, in fact, to have grown more intense. Curtly, he reasoned that this was because he hadn't been with any woman since her and his need was what had grown stronger. Moving closer, he sought her lips with his. She tasted even more delicious than he remembered.

Lisa made no struggle to hold her senses in check. She knew it would be futile. *Just think of this as a fantasy that won't last,* she ordered, releasing herself to the experience.

Slade ran his hand downward from her shoulder over the soft curves of her body to the hem of the short cotton nightgown she was wearing. Then, working his way upward beneath the fabric, he smiled to himself. She was wearing nothing more. As familiar as he was with her body, he still found it excitingly new to his touch...an adventure to be sought and savored.

Lisa wanted to purr as he worked her nightgown upward, his rough calloused hands sending currents of electricity through her until her body tingled with pleasure. When he had worked the gown as high as he could while she lay on her back, he wrapped his arms around her and rolled onto his back, carrying her with him.

Lying on top of him, her body was aware of every inch of contact from the hard musculature of his chest and thighs to his ready maleness. Her breath locked in her lungs as desire caused every fiber of her being to vibrate with anticipation.

Slade's mouth left hers long enough for him to slide the nightgown over her head and off completely. Her breasts, her stomach, her legs, her womanliness all pressed against him and he reveled in the soft, smooth texture of her skin. He wanted her now and he was not certain he could wait. Then she moved, lifting herself until she could accept him.

Lisa wanted his fullness to fill her but forced herself to receive him with slow deliberateness. Feeling his heart pounding beneath the palm of her hand, she was glad she'd remembered how much he'd enjoyed savoring this moment of joining.

The velvet feel of her as she allowed him entry was so erotic Slade could barely breathe. His hands encased her buttocks when he was finally fully within and for a long moment he simply held her there, pressed tightly to him, luxuriating in the feel of their union. Then knowing he could not control himself for long, he began to move, massaging them both in sensual rhythm.

"You feel too good. I can't prolong this," he apologized, increasing his pace, moving with the fervor of a man lost to physical desire.

Lisa made no response. Her vocal cords refused to work. Her whole body was centered on their rhythm. She was moving with him now, her heart pounding so loudly she could hear it. Her blood flowed like lava, then like the cap of a volcano bursting from the flow built up within, her body trembled violently and her womanliness pulsated as she climaxed.

Slade joined her at the apex, marveling at how attuned their bodies were to one another. Again he pressed her to him, continuing to hold them united even as they began their descent.

Lisa rested her head on his shoulder and let her senses be filled with the feel of her body lying on his. When he began to massage her again and then moved lower to her thighs, deep within, the fire they had just sated wanted to flame to life again.

"I have missed you," he murmured in her ear, amazed by how much he wanted to take her again right then. He grinned with amusement at himself. It was ridiculous to think he could be ready so quickly. Then in the next instant, the grin vanished as he realized he was hardening.

Lisa felt him growing stronger and without hesitation accepted him. "Apparently, it has been too long for both of us," she breathed in his ear as they began moving once again in rhythm, each caressing the other, rekindling the embers that had not even had a chance to cool.

Lisa lay in bed the next morning staring up at the ceiling. She was barely aware of her mild soreness from their exertions of the night before. Her mind was still boggled by the intensity with which their bodies had craved each other. Unleashed, uninhibited, animal passion was the only way to describe it. But then, the physical side of their relationship had always been good.

"I didn't wear you out too much, did I?"

She turned her head to see Slade, raised up on an elbow, regarding her with concern. "I'll admit, I'm a little tired this morning." She grinned. "But I'll live."

He smiled. "It's good to have you back in my bed."

She read the camaraderie on his face. He was willing to be her friend and her lover, but she also saw the shadow deep in his eyes that told her that the barrier between her and his heart remained intact. A sharp jab of disappointment pierced her. *So what did you expect?* she chided herself as she rose and headed to the bathroom for a shower.

Tears of frustration welled in Lisa's eyes as she stood under the cascading water. She wanted to hold her son in her arms so badly they ached. Now they were back to square one. A sudden thought occurred to her. Brushing away the tears, she finished her shower quickly. Coming out of the bathroom, she said, "Maybe one of the people I put in jail in Texas hired someone to kill me or has a family member who wants me dead."

Slade nodded. "I'll have Boyd look into it, but two years is a long time to wait for revenge if you're not planning to do it yourself."

The tears again welled in her eyes. "I want to see my son."

"Our son," he reminded her. "And I want the three of us to be a family. After last night, you can't deny that the physical attraction between us is as strong as ever. We can make this marriage work."

She met his gaze levelly. "To be honest, I don't feel married to you. I feel like what we have is a legal affair and a part of me wants to make it work while another part is telling me to run as fast and as far from you as possible."

"I promise you, I'll do what I can to make you happy," Slade said gruffly.

Within the boundaries you've set, Lisa added to herself. Out loud, she said, "What will make me happy right now is to find out who is after me and lock them away."

"While Boyd is checking on any Texas connection, you and I are going to start with your first case and work through every one of them. You'll be seeing Andy soon."

The mention of her son's name brought back the flood of tears and this time they spilled out. Lisa brushed angrily at the salty water streaming down her cheeks. "I can't believe I'm crying. I've never been a whiner."

Slade was surprised, too. He'd never seen her break down like this before. Pulling her into his arms, he said firmly, "We're going to get to the bottom of this. I promise you that."

Lisa had always tried to hide her weaker side from him, but her control was gone. Burying her face in his shoulder, she cried. The solid, secure feel of him soothed her. And, in spite of the fact that he was determined to keep a barrier between his heart and hers, she found his presence comforting and reassuring. Her crying lessened until there were only intermittent sobs.

Slade dropped a light kiss on the top of her head. "I think we need to go get something to eat, then we'll head back to your office."

Her emotional outburst over, Lisa flushed with embarrassment. Crying in front of him had been one thing she'd promised herself she would never do. Straightening away from him, she said stiffly, "I'm sorry. I don't know what got into me."

"It's all right," Slade assured her. "We all have our weak moments."

That brought a disbelieving look to her face. "I find it very hard to believe you have weak moments."

His mouth quirked into a crooked grin. "I'm just better at controlling them."

"You are the master when it comes to holding your emotions in check," she conceded.

Several hours later Lisa sat staring at the stack of files in front of her. So far they hadn't discovered any really promising suspects. Her vision blurred and in her mind's eye she saw her son rushing into her arms. "I need to talk to Andy," she said abruptly.

Slade nodded. "We'll get out of here and find a phone."

They drove around for a while until they were satisfied they weren't being followed, then Slade pulled into the parking lot of a plush hotel and they went inside.

Lisa found a phone in a secluded corner.

"I want to speak to him, too," Slade said as she dialed the ranch.

Lisa had known he would. He never passed up a chance to speak to his son and for Andy's sake she was glad. Satisfied that all the members of her family were comfortable and still feeling welcome at the ranch, she spoke to Andy for several minutes, then turned the phone over to Slade and watched his features soften with pleasure. That he had so quickly bonded with their son caused an uneasy twinge and she was forced to face an uncomfortable truth…it was very possible that even if he had no shield around his heart, all he would ever feel for her was friendship. Maybe that was why he'd been comfortable having a relationship with her in the first place. He liked her but knew he would never be in danger of falling in love with her.

Catching an unusual edge in Slade's voice, she concentrated on his end of the conversation. He'd finished talking to Andy and was talking to his mother. She couldn't figure out what was going on because his end of the conversation was mostly single words, but she could tell that whatever he was being told was of real interest to him.

"Our son and my great-grandmother, Morning Hawk, appear to have bonded strongly," Slade said with a bemused expression as he hung up.

"My mother mentioned that the two of them seem to enjoy each other's company." From somewhere deep in her memory, she recalled Slade saying that his great-grandmother could be difficult and unpredictable. "Could that be a problem?"

Slade grinned. "No. It's good. Morning Hawk was giving in to age, talking about meeting the Great Spirit and being reunited with her ancestors. Now she has a new interest that has restored her zest for life."

Lisa read the relief on his face and realized, that in spite of how difficult his great-grandmother could be, he'd been very worried about her. "Then I'm glad she and Andy have become fast friends."

Slade nodded and cupped her face in his hands. "I'm getting cross-eyed from reading files. How about if we forget about killers for the rest of the day? I can think of a much better way to spend our time."

Her body flamed to life beneath his touch. "My mind is a blur. I could use a few hours of relaxation."

Slade heard the heat in her voice and it pleased him that her need for him was as great as his need for her.

For a brief moment the knowledge that he didn't love her caused Lisa to again wish she could play a little harder to get, then she silently laughed at herself. It was too late for that.

After checking in at the front desk, Slade slipped an arm around her waist as they rode up in the elevator. Just his touch was enough to drive her to distraction. By the time they stepped into their room, she wanted to rip his clothes off. But a loud growl from her stomach reminded her that they hadn't had any lunch.

Hearing her stomach made Slade realize how hungry he was. The problem was that he was as hungry for her as he was for food. One step at a time, he told himself, and picked up the room service menu from the desk and handed it to her. "So what would you like?"

You was the answer that popped into her head, but she managed to swallow it back and forced her eyes to focus on the selections. She chose the salmon and handed the menu back to him.

Hanging up the phone after placing their order, Slade said, "They said it would take about forty-five minutes."

He was looking at her with that "wanting you" look in his eyes and her body blazed. "I suppose we'll have to find some way to kill the time. Do you have any ideas?''

''Just one,'' he returned huskily, reaching her in a long stride.

Without any preliminaries, they began to undress one another.

In spite of her familiarity with his body, the excitement of fresh adventure raged through Lisa. She loved touching him, running her hands over his chest, tasting the sweetness of his skin. And his body's response told her that he was enjoying their tryst as much as she was.

Lifting her onto the bed, Slade experienced a rush of possessiveness. The intensity of it caused a jolt of uneasiness. They were compatible companions and friends, that was all, he told himself. He would let his feelings for her go no further. Satisfied he had his emotions in check once again, he concentrated on the physical side of their union, reveling in the pleasure she gave him and in doing all he could to please her as much.

When he entered her, Lisa felt as if they were truly one and realized that when she was with him like this, it felt so incredibly right. It was as if their bodies had been made for one another. Delicious erotic pleasure flowed through her filling her senses until her awareness of their uniting was all that existed for her. It had a power all its own that claimed every fiber of her being. Then suddenly her breath locked in her lungs and she joined Slade at the zenith.

Sated, lying beside him, Lisa knew this was where she belonged. She just wished Slade would allow her to become more than just a compatible companion. She took a long steadying breath. The trick was to not fall in love with him again. ''I can do that,'' she murmured out loud, using the sound of her voice to add strength to this vow.

"You can do what?" Slade asked.

She turned to look him in the eye. "I can stay as emotionally immune to you as you are to me."

He smiled. "Then I know we can make this marriage work."

Lisa told herself she should feel empowered or relieved or some other positive emotion. This time, she was setting the boundaries. But instead, she felt a small but deep circle of hollowness inside.

Chapter Ten

Slade's cell phone rang a little after eight the next morning.

It was Detective Overson. "I'd like for you and Miss Gray to come down to my office," he requested. "There's a woman here with a pretty farfetched story. But she swears it's true."

"It's Mrs. Logan," Slade corrected him, then asked, "Are you telling me you know who's after Lisa?"

"Maybe. I need Mrs. Logan to verify some facts before we can take this seriously."

"We'll be there as soon as possible."

Lisa stared at Slade as he hung up. "Was that Overson? Does he know who's after me?"

"Maybe. We need to get to his office."

A short while later, they entered the detective's office to discover a woman who looked to be in her early sixties. She was shaking and Lisa was afraid she was going to faint or, even worse, have a stroke or a heart attack.

"This is Mrs. Dorothy Parkens." Overson made the introduction.

Tears welled in the woman's eyes. "I really don't know how I got mixed up in this." Wringing her hands, she looked into Lisa's face. "I am so sorry for all that you have been through. I thought they were just joking around." The tears escaped and rolled down her cheeks. "It's like a nightmare."

Good description, Lisa mused silently.

"You know who's been trying to kill Lisa?" Slade asked curtly.

Dorothy nodded her head. "It's like I told the detective, I was out of town until just a few days ago. That was when I found out what was going on. At first I couldn't believe it. Then, when I realized it was real, I got scared. They said that if I didn't go along with them, they would kill George, that's my husband, and frame me for it. I haven't slept. I knew I had to do something to stop them. My conscience wouldn't allow me to let them go around killing people so I made sure I wasn't followed and came here."

Lisa was finding it hard to believe that this little old lady who looked like someone's grandmother was mixed up with killers, but she was clearly very upset and scared. "Who are *they*?"

"Claire Blout and Paula Morgan."

"Claire Blout? Milton Blout's wife?" Lisa pictured the middle-class, fifty-seven-year-old woman, a little on the stout side with graying hair. She looked sweet and innocent, like someone's favorite aunt. "Why would she want me dead? And I don't even know a Paula Morgan."

Dorothy read the disbelief on Lisa's face. "I know it sounds ridiculous, but it's the truth. It all began with water aerobics."

Slade frowned at the woman with an expression that suggested he thought her elevator didn't go all the way to the top. "'Water aerobics'?"

Dorothy's expression turned grim and she nodded her head. "That's where we met, Claire, Paula and me. They found me crying in the locker room. I needed someone to talk to and I was too embarrassed to talk to family. I had discovered that my husband had had a long string of affairs. He'd had a serious heart attack. He'd always handled the money and we'd always lived frugally...saving for our old age, he said. But the truth was he'd been spending tons on his other women. Anyway, he realized that if he did survive, he was in such bad shape I'd have to take over the finances, at least for a while, and I'd know something was wrong as soon as I saw what was coming in and what we had. And he needed me to nurse him. So he confessed and begged me to forgive him. I don't believe in divorce so I really didn't have a choice. Claire and Paula helped me through that difficult time."

Lisa found herself wondering if Slade would ever cheat on her. The fact that he didn't love her made that a possibility. *This is not the time or place to be thinking about him and your marriage,* she scoffed at herself. *This is the time and place to be concerned with whether you will live to have a future with anyone.* "I'm sorry your marriage turned out so badly, but would you please tell me why Claire Blout and Paula Morgan want me dead?" Lisa wanted the woman to get her back to their original subject.

Dorothy sighed and brushed the tears from her face. "Bad marriages. That's the reason. Since his heart attack, I've taken good care of George. But the love is gone. I can't get rid of the sense of betrayal."

"That must be very difficult to live with," Lisa sympathized. Just the thought of Slade cheating on her while he was sharing her bed was painful and she wasn't even under the delusion that he was in love with her.

"It is and Claire and Paula are both in sort of the same boat. They're caught up in marriages they would prefer to be out of. Claire wants more excitement in her life. She feels that Milton is making her feel old before her time. And Paula is married to an abusive drunk. We started having coffee regularly after aerobics and venting our anger. Talking about how furious I was with George helped me get rid of some of my rage. Oh, I'll admit, I'll always be angry with him, but not enough to kill him."

"Kill him? You actually considered killing your husband?" It was Slade who spoke.

Dorothy gave him a dry look. "Don't you think that we women care as much about fidelity as men do? Men are always shooting their wives when the wives cheat on them." Defiance flashed in her eyes. "I suppose you think it would be all right for a man to have a fling once in a while."

"No. I believe that a man should live by his word."

Lisa heard the commitment in Slade's voice and knew that as long as they were married, he would never cheat on her. But then, why should he? His heart belonged to Claudette. She, Lisa, was merely a way for him to satisfy his physical needs. *Stop thinking about him!* she ordered herself, and focused her full attention on Dorothy.

Dorothy was looking up at Slade with admiration on her face. "Too bad my George didn't feel that way." Her grim expression returned. "But I just couldn't kill him."

"I'm confused," Lisa said. "What has you killing George or not killing George got to do with me?"

"It wasn't just me killing George. It was all of us

getting rid of our husbands. Claire saw this movie about these wives who got together and killed each other's husbands. Since none of them had any obvious reason to kill whoever they killed, they weren't suspected. In the movie it was only some silly, contrived accident that led the police to them.''

Lisa stared at this grandmotherly looking woman in disbelief. ''The three of you plotted to kill each other's husbands?''

''I didn't actually think Claire and Paula were serious. I thought we were just fantasizing.'' Her eyes pleaded with Lisa for understanding. ''Wouldn't you think it was just talk? We're three old women. We've all lived a fairly routine life. At least, as far as I know, we have. How in the world was I supposed to know Claire and Paula were homicidal lunatics?''

''What you're telling me doesn't make any sense,'' Lisa said coolly. ''Claire didn't need to kill Milton. He was giving her a divorce.'' Her gaze bore into Dorothy, daring the woman to continue with this lie. ''And she was the one who called off the divorce because she still loves him. I heard her over the phone. The two of them are like a couple of lovebirds.''

''Claire is a very good actress. But I can assure you that calling off the divorce had nothing to do with love. It had everything to do with money. Claire found out how little she would get. That's why she called it off.''

Lisa had handled a couple of cases where the woman had decided to stay married simply because she'd have been nearly destitute if she'd gone through with the divorce. It wasn't a healthy situation. But Claire and Milton had sounded so happy.

''Claire Blout told you that she was remaining with Milton so that she could kill him and get everything?''

"Not at first. We'd met for tea at a place outside of town...her choice. She said she'd decided to call off the divorce because she refused to give up money she felt she'd earned. Then she said that it would really be nice if Milton had an accident and died. That way she'd have her freedom, all of their assets and his life insurance policy to boot. Then, both Paula and I said that we wouldn't miss our spouses, either." Dorothy stiffened in defiance. "But, I would never really have considered doing anything to bring about George's demise. I was just venting my anger. Anyway, that's when Claire brought up the movie." Dorothy looked panicky and tears again welled in her eyes. "She and Paula got to figuring out ways we could get rid of each other's husbands. I joined in. I thought we were just joking around."

"How did Lisa figure into all of this?" Slade demanded.

"When Claire told Milton that the reason she'd wanted the divorce was because she'd felt neglected and he confessed that he'd been so jealous he'd hired a private detective to see if she had a boyfriend, Claire realized that Miss Gray—"

"It's Mrs. Logan now," Slade interjected.

"Oh." Fear showed on Dorothy's face as if she expected him to seek vengeance on her at that moment.

"Please go on with your story," Lisa encouraged gently.

The woman's gaze swung to her. "Yes. As I was saying, Claire realized that you would probably have seen the three of us together and might put three and three together and figure out what was going on. So Claire and Paula decided they had to get rid of you first."

Slade glowered at the woman. "Why didn't you come forward when Lisa was shot?"

"I didn't know about it. Like I said, I've been out of town. I didn't even know Claire and Paula were serious about killing their husbands until I got back. About a month ago George was finally well enough to travel. I'd always wanted to go to Europe and to make amends he'd taken me. We were gone for four weeks. When I got back, Claire told me that they were going to put *our* plan into action as soon as they'd gotten rid of Mrs. Logan. I couldn't believe they were really going through with it. I tried to reason with them, but they said it was too late and they told me how they'd already tried to get rid of her. That was when they threatened me and insisted I had to go along with them."

"Claire Blout seemed so normal," Lisa muttered.

"She is, mostly," Dorothy said. "She and Paula are just a bit greedier, or maybe just more willing than the rest of us to go to extremes to get what they want."

"Who took the shot at Lisa?" Slade asked, wanting to piece together the puzzle as completely as possible.

"Someone they hired out of one of those soldier of fortune magazines. Claire was furious when he refused to finish the job."

Lisa regarded her skeptically. "Hired killers don't usually stop before the job is done. It's part of their code."

"He hadn't planned on everyone thinking he'd shot the wrong person. Instead of just having the local police looking for him, he had the FBI or whatever agency was protecting that gangster after him, too. And then, because the hit hadn't been sanctioned by the mob, they put a contract out on him. At least, that was what he told Claire. Anyway, he took off and they decided they would do the job themselves."

"So you're telling us that these ladies tried to run Lisa down, built the bomb and cut the brake line?"

Dorothy nodded. "They found out how to build the bomb from the Internet. And they used a car maintenance manual to find out about the brake line. Paula had seen it done on television and figured it might work."

"And how have they been tracking us?" Slade asked.

"Through your credit and bank cards. Claire enjoys hacking. She's done it for ages. And, during an earlier episode in her marriage when she'd decided she wanted her own spending money, she'd worked for a while for one of those companies that checks people's credit ratings. Somehow she managed to figure out how to actually access individual credit card records and with the way transactions are so quickly transferred to your account these days, she could follow you pretty closely. And I think they might have access to your cell phone records, as well. But I'm not sure about that. Paula said something about having a nephew who worked for one of the cell phone companies and that she was going to find out from him if there was a way of accessing accounts. She said he liked to show off and, if there was a way, she was sure she could trick him into showing her."

Slade sat back and shook his head. "Women who you'd think were spending their time planning church socials or family gatherings, plotting murder to get rid of their husbands. It's scary." He turned to Overson. "So what do we do now?"

"That depends on Mrs. Parkens."

Dorothy turned a questioning look on the detective. "I've told you everything."

"Your word and a dollar will get us a cup of coffee at the courthouse," he replied.

"You don't believe me?"

"It's not that I don't believe you, but we need proof."

"I'll take a lie detector test."

"That's inadmissible in court."

Panic entered Dorothy's voice. "I don't have any proof. I was just trying to do what I thought was right. Are you going to try to frame this whole business on me just because you need someone to arrest? Well, if you do, Mrs. Logan is going to remain in danger."

Worried that the woman would suddenly become uncooperative, Lisa stepped in. "It isn't that Detective Overson doesn't trust you, it's just that he needs physical proof."

Overson smiled his best friendly smile. "I know you've taken a risk coming to us, and I'm not doubting you. But I need to ask you to do something else for us."

Dorothy's panic subsided a little, but her guardedness remained. "What?"

"If you would wear a wire and get the women to incriminate themselves on tape, we'd have a case."

Dorothy paled. "They'll kill me if they find out."

"If you don't help us, you'll end up with innocent blood on your hands," Slade said.

Dorothy looked pleadingly at Detective Overson. "Isn't there some other way? They scare me."

"It's the only sure way of catching them," Overson said.

Dorothy's gaze again traveled around the small group. "I guess I don't really have a choice." Her eyes begged them to tell her that she did.

"I don't see any other way." Lisa broke the silence that had fallen over the room.

Overson smiled encouragingly. "I'll have men guarding you constantly from the moment you leave here. And I'll have Mrs. Blout and Mrs. Morgan under surveillance twenty-four hours a day."

"I've always lived such a quiet life. I can't believe I got myself mixed up in this," Dorothy groaned.

Overson turned his attention to Slade and Lisa. "Now that we know who we're after, I'd suggest that you two leave town. Get out of the line of fire. Wouldn't want these amateurs to get lucky just when we're closing in on them."

"We'll be out of here on the next plane," Slade vowed.

Lisa thanked Dorothy for coming forward. Slade added his thanks and they left.

Driving to the airport, Lisa couldn't help thinking that living in a bad marriage could have had as much to do with these middle-aged women going over the edge as greed. And she wondered what living in Claudette's shadow would do to her. Would she become bitter and resentful? She didn't like picturing herself turning into a frustrated shrew.

"Penny for your thoughts," Slade said.

She glanced toward him. They were stopped at a light and he was studying her with concern.

"You look like a woman with a heavy load on her mind," he elaborated.

"I am," she conceded. "But it's my load to bear and for now, I'm going to bear it alone."

Slade reached over and gently caressed her cheek. "I want you to understand that I'll always be here for you. You don't have to bear any load on your own."

His touch wove through her like a current of warmth and she knew the resistance she'd been attempting to keep in place was useless. He held her heart in his hands. He always had. But reading his face, she saw only friendship there.

Chapter Eleven

Lisa shifted uneasily in her seat as they neared the Logan ranch. During the flight to Lubbock, the worry that Slade's mother and other members of his family might think she was a gold digger who had gotten pregnant on purpose so that she could bind Slade to her and as a consequence benefit from his family's wealth came back to haunt her.

Again she argued that going off on her own and not contacting him until she realized that Andy might be orphaned should convince them that was not her intention. By the time she and Slade turned off the main road onto the long driveway leading to the ranch house, she'd come close to convincing herself that this was a needless worry. Still, she remained tense. His family had to know that Slade would never have married her if it hadn't been for Andy's existence.

As they pulled up in front of the ranch house her worries about how his family would receive her were pushed to the back of her mind by the sight of her son. He was

sitting on the front porch with her mother, her aunt and
an ancient-looking Native American woman who she
guessed was Slade's great-grandmother. Seeing her
climbing out of the car, Andy headed to the porch steps.
Her mother caught up with him and helped him down
the short flight. They reached the bottom at the same time
Lisa did. Squatting, she wrapped her arms around Andy
and nuzzled his neck. "I missed you," she said.

He giggled and hugged her back. Excitement gleaming
in his eyes, he lifted his face so that they were nose to
nose. "Mee. Coowbooy."

The thought of him on his pony, brought its usual rush
of panic. Trying to not let this natural fear of a mother
for her son show, she smiled back. "I know."

Slade waited until Lisa had had a couple of minutes to
reunite with their child, then said, "Howdy, son."

Andy turned to him, frowned for a second as if trying
to place the man, then smiled and allowed Slade to pick
him up.

That brief second when Andy hadn't recognized him
cut through Slade like a knife and he vowed his son
would never not know him again.

Lisa, too, had seen the momentary hesitation on her
son's face and the tensing of Slade's jaw that told her he
hadn't liked it. Slade, she knew now for certain, would
do anything to be a father to his child…anything but
open his heart to her.

"It's good to have you home, big brother," a younger
version of Slade called, coming around the house from
the direction of the barns and stables. Without waiting
for a response, Jess gave Slade a slap on the shoulder
and extended his hand to Lisa. "And it's good to meet
you. You've got a mighty fine son there."

The friendliness on his face was genuine and Lisa

smiled as she accepted the handshake. "Thanks, I think so."

"Going to make one hell of a cowboy. Sits that pony as if he was born to it," Jess added, ruffling Andy's hair.

"I've been so worried about you," Helen said, giving her daughter a welcoming hug.

Past her mother's shoulder, Lisa saw Ester helping the elderly Apache woman down the porch steps. And, as her mother released her, she noticed that both Slade and Jess had become wary.

"You have given this family a child to be proud of," the old woman said when she reached Lisa. With a loving expression on her face, she patted Andy on the arm, then returned her attention to Lisa. "I am Morning Hawk. And I have something for you. It is to keep you safe." From the pocket of the fringed doeskin tunic dress she wore, she extracted a single strand of beads with a small carved wooden bear dangling from them. "Bend down," she ordered. When Lisa obeyed, she slipped the beads around her neck. This task completed, she turned and walked back to the porch.

The lack of even a hint of a smile on the elderly woman's face told Lisa that although she didn't want any harm to come to her, she was reserving judgment on her.

"You have to get used to her," Helen whispered into her daughter's ear. "When we got here, Slade's mother and grandmother warned us that she could be difficult at times, but so far she's behaved herself. She hasn't said much to Ester and me but she watches over Andy like a protective hen. Actually, they all do."

Lisa wasn't surprised by this news. She'd known how strongly Slade's people felt about family ties. She also knew how protective they were of one another.

"So you're finally here." A woman's voice rang out from the direction of the house.

Lisa saw two women come out the front door and head toward them.

Reaching the group, the women gave Slade hugs, then turned to Lisa. The younger spoke. "I'm Slade's mother, White Moon."

Lisa noted that there was a guardedness about her friendliness as there was the older woman with her. Clearly, as Slade's great-grandmother, they, too, were reserving judgment.

"And this is my mother, Evening Flower." White Moon introduced the woman beside her.

Andy, who had been perched comfortably on Slade's arm, suddenly held his arms out to Lisa. "Mommy," he demanded.

Realizing that the boy has sensed the tension in the women toward Lisa, Slade cast his mother a reproving look. She merely shrugged as if to say she was his mother and it was her duty to protect him.

Lisa was glad to take possession of her son. Just holding his hand with him standing by her side gave her courage. "I'm pleased to meet you." Mentally she congratulated herself for managing to keep any stiffness out of her voice. Then with genuine gratitude, she added, "And I want to thank you for providing a haven for my family."

"It is my understanding that we are all family now," White Moon said, continuing to study her narrowly. "Slade told us that the two of you are married."

"Yes," Lisa confirmed.

"As it should be." White Moon made it sound as if there had been no other choice. She turned her gaze to Slade. "The papers you requested me to have our lawyer draw up to make you legally Andy's father and have his name changed to Logan are in the study. When you have looked them over, you are to call him and make arrangements for them to be signed. Lisa will have to be present. Her signature will be needed on the documents, as well.''

Lisa mentally scoffed at herself for being even the tiniest bit surprised that Slade had already made arrangements for the legalities to be completed. He'd always been a man of action. What bothered her was the way White Moon continued to regard her with suspicion. ''Do you have any doubts about Slade being Andy's father?'' she asked bluntly.

''No. I am simply worried about your intentions for the future. It is obvious this marriage between you and my son was done merely for the child's sake. That is not a good basis for any marriage and certainly not for a happy one.''

''Our marriage and what happens in it, is between Lisa and me,'' Slade interjected, his tone warning his mother that she was treading where she was not welcome.

''I am merely concerned about you and about Andy.'' Her gaze turned on Lisa. ''Since we are speaking bluntly...I don't want to see my son trapped in an unhappy marriage or Andy caught in a struggle between the two of you.''

Lisa couldn't blame her. She was Slade's mother. It was only natural for her to be protective of him. And she was glad the woman showed honest concern for Andy. At least he had been fully welcomed into the Logan clan.

''My daughter is a good and decent woman. You don't have to worry about her doing anything to harm your son,'' Helen cut in tersely. ''And she most certainly would never cause Andy harm or grief.''

Evening Flower moved next to her daughter in a show

of support for White Moon while Helen moved closer to
Lisa and Ester took a stance on the other side of her
niece. A sense of war filled the air. That was not what
Lisa wanted.

"I understand your concern," she said, meeting White
Moon's gaze levelly, then casting glances at both her aunt
and her mother that ordered them to cease and desist.
"But I assure you, I have no intention of causing anyone
any harm. I never wanted to foist myself on Slade. I
would have continued to raise Andy on my own if I
hadn't realized that one day he could find himself alone
in this world."

"I didn't mean to imply that I am sorry you told my
son about his child. Andy should know his father and his
father's family."

What she hadn't said caused Lisa's shoulders to
straighten with pride. "I know Slade would never have
married me if it wasn't for Andy and I have no intention
of making his life miserable by forcing him to continue
in a union that he does not want."

Slade glowered at his mother. "I'm the one who insisted on the marriage and I'm the one who wants it to
continue."

White Moon faced him without flinching. "Do you
love her?"

"I care for her and I respect her. Now, it's been a long
day. We'd like to go inside and freshen up."

"I think we'll just take Lisa and Andy and go to a
motel," Helen said, wrapping an arm around her daughter's shoulders.

Evening Flower placed an arm around White Moon's
shoulders. "I apologize for my daughter. She is very protective of all of her sons, but especially of Slade. He's

been deeply wounded. She only wishes him happiness, the kind that can only be found with a true love."

"I warned you that they were being too polite, too sweet," Ester hissed at Helen. "And all those questions about Lisa. They were looking for something to discredit her."

"I just don't want to see my son hurt," White Moon snapped.

"I can take care of myself." Slade scowled at his mother. He'd known it would be an uphill battle to convince Lisa to stay with him. His mother's overly protective attitude was not helping.

"Enough!" It was Morning Hawk who spoke, her voice carrying sharp authority. She turned to her daughter and granddaughter. "You don't want to see Slade hurt." She turned to Helen and Ester. "And you don't want to see Lisa hurt." Her gaze swept all four women. "I know my daughter and granddaughter and I have been observing Lisa's aunt and mother for the past days. You are all good people with righteous intentions. But Slade and Lisa are adults. They will make their own decisions and their own mistakes." She made a sweeping gesture toward the house. "We should all go inside. Dinner will be ready soon."

Helen and Ester stiffened their stance, remaining immobile. As for her part, Lisa was uncertain. She was in no mood to spend time in an enemy camp. Even more, she didn't want Andy to feel caught in the midst of a battle.

Jess shook his head at his mother. "I thought we'd agreed to honor Slade's wishes and trust his judgment."

"I told you I knew what I was doing." Slade fought hard to control his temper. He knew his mother had his best interests at heart but he'd thought he'd made it clear to her that Lisa could be trusted.

White Moon took a deep breath and exhaled. "I am sorry," she said stiffly to the entire gathering, then directed her attention to Lisa and her family. "Please stay."

"Mommy?"

Lisa looked at her son to see confusion on his face and tears of fear brimming in his eyes. "It's all right, sweetheart," she soothed. "We're just clearing the air."

"I still vote we leave," Ester insisted.

Morning Hawk laid a hand on her arm. "If you were standing in my granddaughter's shoes would you not be concerned?"

"Well, she doesn't have anything to worry about when it comes to Lisa. Anyone should be proud to have her as a daughter-in-law," Ester returned.

"And are you without reservations about having Slade as a son-in-law?" Morning Hawk countered.

Ester shifted uneasily. "I don't know him well enough to be certain about him."

"So it would seem we must all get to know each other better," the elderly woman said.

Ester remained mute, continuing to look unconvinced.

Lisa's jaw firmed. For Andy's sake she had to try to develop a comfortable or at least polite relationship with Slade's mother and grandmother. "We'll stay the night and see how things go."

"Thank you," White Moon said with honest gratitude.

It was clear to Lisa that the woman did regret coming very close to chasing her off. Well, maybe not her as much as Andy. White Moon motioned for the others to precede her into the house. "Please, come inside. The meal is almost ready."

Ester looked disgruntled and Helen uncertain of what was the right thing to do, but when Lisa started toward the door with Andy, they accompanied her.

Slade hung back and Jess stayed with him. "Is the perimeter secured?" he asked in lowered tones.

"I've got men posted in a full circle around us. Nothing is going to get through."

"We'll keep them there until we get word that those lunatic women are under lock and key," Slade said.

Jess nodded his agreement.

Slade watched grimly as the women disappeared into the house. "Do you think Mother will behave or do we need to post guards inside, as well?"

Jess placed an arm around his brother's shoulder. "She's just worried about you. For ten years you've been nursing a wounded heart and she knows the wound is still festering. She was hoping you'd find a woman who could heal it. Instead you've been forced into a marriage for the sake of your son."

"I wasn't forced," Slade growled.

Jess held up his hands in surrender. "Hey, I'm on your side. I just want you to be happy. You're living proof that being too much in love can be harmful. So maybe being married to a woman you're merely fond of will work a whole lot better."

"That's my way of thinking," Slade replied, feeling confident in his ability to keep his emotions toward Lisa just that...fond of but not in love with.

Chapter Twelve

"I want to apologize for my behavior and to welcome Lisa to our family," White Moon said as they all gathered at the dinner table a short while later.

"Ester and I understand your concern for your son. We're just as concerned about Lisa," Helen replied, clearly determined to let Slade's family know that he was under as much scrutiny by her and Ester as Lisa was by them.

Not wanting the conversation to follow that path into the brier patch again, Lisa interrupted to ask Jess how Andy's riding lessons were going.

"He's got good balance. 'Course his legs will have to grow a bit more before he can be on his own," Jess replied, the expression of a proud uncle on his face.

"I would think so," Helen said sternly.

Lisa glanced toward White Moon, expecting trouble. Instead the woman frowned with parental authority at both of her sons. "I don't want you pushing him too fast.

His feet should fit firmly in the stirrups before you allow him to even walk the pony without someone at his side.''

"Yes, ma'am," they both answered in unison.

The servile tone of these two big men toward the much smaller woman brought a smile to Lisa's lips and she noted that the corners of her mother's and her aunt's mouths curved up slightly, as well.

"I'm interested in hearing more about these women who have been trying to kill you," Evening Flower said. "Slade has relayed only the barest of details."

Glad to have something to talk about other than subjects that might lead to tension, Lisa launched into a recitation of their meeting with Dorothy Parkens.

"It doesn't seem real," she finished. "I tailed Claire Blout for two weeks. She seemed like a perfectly normal middle-aged woman. I would never have pegged her for a killer."

White Moon's gaze leveled on Lisa and Slade. "It would seem that it was their unhappy marriages that drove them to this extreme."

Slade frowned at his mother. "A lot of people have unhappy marriages but they simply get divorced. These women were greedy."

The concern on White Moon's face increased. "Greed can be a very nasty emotion."

The uneasy glance she cast in Lisa's direction told Lisa she was thinking about Slade's comfortable income. Lisa's shoulders stiffened with indignation. Glancing toward her mother and her aunt, she realized they, too, were following White Moon's train of thought because both were turning beet-red with anger.

Jess shook his head at his mother while Evening Flower appeared at a loss for words and Morning Hawk scowled darkly at her granddaughter.

Placing an arm around Lisa's shoulders, Slade looked his mother in the eye. "You're way off base if you think that Lisa would harm anyone out of greed. I trust her with my life."

White Moon flushed with embarrassment, her expression saying that even she was shocked by what she'd just suggested. "I didn't mean to imply she would," she said hastily, dropping her gaze to her food.

Lisa had been willing to forgive the woman's earlier behavior because she knew White Moon was concerned about her son, but this was an outrage. "Andy is finished and I've lost my appetite," she said, rising. "If you will excuse us."

Slade rose, too, and lifted Andy from his chair.

Taking her son by his hand, Lisa continued through the house and out the back door. Once outside, she let him pull her toward the corral where his pony was housed.

"I know that down deep my mother doesn't really believe you would do me any harm," Slade said, falling into step beside her.

"She went too far," Lisa returned through clenched teeth. "Way too far. I never asked you to marry me. Tomorrow, you call your lawyer and arrange for a divorce because until I'm free of you, I'll have to worry that every time you even stub a toe, your mother will blame me."

"I won't blame you," a woman's panicked voice sounded from behind them.

Lisa whirled around and saw White Moon hurrying toward them, a stricken look on her face. Reaching them, she faced Lisa squarely. "Of all my sons, Slade is the one I've worried about the most. I know I was way out of line, but ever since he told me that he intended to try to make a go of your marriage, I've been deeply concerned. You have no idea how crushed he was when Claudette died. He just crumbled." Her jaw set in a hard line. "I wanted him to find someone who would mend the wound Claudette left behind. But perhaps it can never be mended. You've given him a wonderful son and for that I am grateful. I just don't want to see the two of you try to make a go of a marriage for your child's sake that neither of you really wants and that will make you both bitter in the end."

Claudette again. "You're right," Lisa said stiffly. "An attempt would be futile and I have no desire to put myself or Slade through it."

Slade caught her by the arm. "We can make it work."

She jerked free. "No, we can't."

"Mommy?" Andy's panicked tone reminded them he was there.

"Let's go say good-night to your pony," she said, turning away from Slade and his mother and continuing on toward the corral. A tear escaped and rolled down her cheek but she waited until she was a distance from them before she brushed it away.

Slade stood glowering at his mother. "You have no idea what you've done."

White Moon stared at him. An expression of understanding suddenly spread over her features. "You love her. Why didn't you tell me that?"

"I don't love her. I like her. We're comfortable together. I enjoy being with her."

"You won't let yourself love her," White Moon corrected. As if it had all become clear to her, her gaze shifted to the woman and child by the corral. "That's why she left, isn't it? She loved you but knew you would never allow yourself to love her." Sympathy for Lisa swept through her. "Then perhaps this is for the best."

"No, it's not," Slade snapped, and stalked toward the corral to join Lisa and Andy.

"I need you to leave me alone for a while," Lisa said when he approached.

"My mother is wrong. We can make a go of our marriage," he said curtly. "We are friends, good friends. That's a better start than a lot of marriages have."

"So we'll end ours better than most, as well. I'll settle for a friendly divorce."

Slade heard the hint of pain in her voice. It was the same hint he'd heard on their last date when she'd said goodbye. Maybe his mother was right. "I'll do whatever will make you happy."

She tightened her chin to keep it from trembling. "Then go contact your lawyer and get the papers drawn up."

Responding to the dismissal in her voice, Slade headed back to the house.

Andy tugged at Lisa's hand. "Mommy?" he asked with concern.

"Mommy's fine," she assured him, squatting down and giving him a hug.

"It's getting chilly out here." Helen's voice sounded from behind them and Lisa turned to see her mother and her aunt coming her way, her mother carrying a jacket for Andy and one for her.

"What happened?" Ester asked bluntly when they reached her.

"Just a little more clearing of the air," Lisa replied, accepting her jacket while her mother took Andy and began putting his jacket on him.

"White Moon came in all contrite and told us she realized she'd been wrong to ever doubt you. Then Slade came stalking in and didn't say a word to anyone. He just went into the study and slammed the door closed.''

"He's contacting his lawyer to have our divorce papers drawn up," Lisa said stiffly.

"So that's why White Moon was so nice," Ester muttered. "She managed to break up your marriage." She glanced at her watch. "In less than six hours."

"She didn't break it up. She merely caused me to face the truth. And," she added, determined to do her part to keep peace between the families, "as I recall, neither of you were happy about my marrying Slade. The both of you knew it was only because of Andy and it wasn't going to last."

"True." Helen shivered and frowned over her shoulder at the ranch house. "I'll be glad to get back home."

Lisa, too, was looking at the ranch house and dreading entering it again. "Would you two take Andy inside and put him to bed?" she requested. "I'd like some time alone."

"Of course." Helen took Andy by the hand and, fastening her free hand around Ester's arm, pulled her along, as well.

Alone, Lisa rested her arms on the wooden railing of the corral and let the tears trickle down her cheeks. The feel of a hand coming to rest on her arm caused her to jump. Jerking her gaze around to see who had intruded on her privacy, she discovered it was Morning Hawk.

"This divorce is wrong. Your tears are proof of it." The elderly woman spoke with the authority of a sage.

Lisa brushed at her cheeks, furious that she'd let anyone see her cry. "No, it isn't. In the end, it will keep a great many more of my tears from spilling."

"You cannot cut Slade out of your life with a piece of paper. He won't allow that. Andy is his son."

"I don't plan to cut him out."

"He will be a good and loyal husband to you. That is more than many women who marry for love end up with."

"I can't stay married to him."

Morning Hawk regarded her sternly. "Slade is a good man. You would be a fool to discard him."

"Discard? You make it sound like I have a choice. I don't." The tears again welled in Lisa's eyes. "If I stay married to him, I will always hope that one day he will open his heart to me. And he won't. I'll grow old and frustrated and, perhaps, even bitter. That won't be good for either of us."

"You could be wrong. Given time, he may open his heart to you."

The tears began to spill again. "You have no idea how much I'd like to believe that, but I learned the hard way that it's not going to happen. When we began our affair, I had hopes that he would learn to love me. He didn't. When I left, he watched me walk away, then went on with his life without any further thought of me. I don't blame him. He told me from the start that he never intended to fall in love again. But it still hurt. I'm not setting myself up for that kind of pain again."

Morning Hawk looked over her shoulder toward the house. "He can be stubborn. It's a strong trait in Logan men." Breathing a resigned sigh, she turned back to Lisa. "But whatever happens between you and Slade, you must always remember that you are family now."

"My son is family," Lisa corrected, certain she would never be anyone other than the woman who gave birth to Slade's child.

Morning Hawk took her hand. "You are family." She gave the hand a squeeze then released it. "And now I will leave you to your solitude."

"Thank you." Watching the elderly Apache make her way back to the house, Lisa doubted the rest of the family felt the same as Morning Hawk. "This is the only solution," she murmured under her breath.

Returning to the house, Lisa hoped to make it to her son's room to see that he was tucked in and then retreat to her room without encountering anyone. But, entering the kitchen, she found her mother, her aunt, Slade's mother and grandmother all sitting around the table. From the united expressions on their faces, it was clear they had come to a truce.

White Moon rose and came toward her. "I am truly sorry this marriage between you and my son is not going to work out."

Lisa noted that the sincerity on her face was genuine.

"Slade is a fool for letting my niece go," Ester mumbled.

Helen nudged her hard. "If it's not meant to be, then it's not meant to be."

Although Lisa had told her mother many times that Slade had not seduced her...that she had been the one to pursue the affair, Lisa had suspected that her mother harbored some animosity toward him. The edge of anger she heard in her mother's voice told her she was right. Clearly, as far as Helen was concerned, Lisa was doing the right thing. "I'm going to check on Andy and then go to bed," she said, continuing through the room.

Entering Andy's room, she stood watching him sleep. "I knew your father was trouble from the start," she murmured under her breath. "But I will never regret having you." She placed a light kiss on his cheek, then went to the room she and Slade had been given.

The sight of his suitcase caused her to freeze. From deep within an intense anger, an anger she had been suppressing all these years, began to build. Picking up the suitcase, she left the room and went in search of Slade. She found him in the study, standing staring out the window. Entering, she set his suitcase down with a thud. "You can find someplace else to bunk," she snapped.

Slade turned to face her. His expression shuttered, he nodded his acceptance of her decision.

Lisa started to leave, but the rage she was feeling was too strong. Kicking the door closed with the heel of her shoe, she turned back. "I know I'm not perfect, but I would have made you a terrific wife," she stormed. Bravado and pride forced her to add, "Someday, when you're old and alone, you're going to regret casting me aside in favor of a ghost."

"It's not that simple."

"I know. I know." She meant to say nothing more, but her anger was still too strong to control. "You don't want to go through the pain of losing a woman you love again. Well, life is full of ups and downs and that's just one of them."

"It isn't just fear." The agony he kept hidden inside etched itself into his features. "I owe Claudette my unwavering allegiance."

Stunned by the anguish she saw on his face, Lisa stared at him in confusion. "You *owe* her?"

"She would be alive today, if it wasn't for me." This confession tore from him, exposing the guilt that had been haunting him all these years.

Her rage was now completely gone. This was a Slade she'd never seen. Sympathy for him swept through her.

"You weren't responsible. She was hit by a drunk driver."

"We'd had a quarrel. I'd been working on a case and she was feeling neglected. She thought I wasn't as attracted to her because she was pregnant. I tried to tell her that I thought she was beautiful, but she was too emotional to listen. She slammed out of the house saying she was going for a drive to cool off. I figured I'd take her someplace special for dinner the next night. I'd made the arrangements and was waiting for her to come home when the call came." He inhaled a terse breath. "I should never have let her get behind the wheel."

"She was legally crossing an intersection. The other driver ran a red light." Lisa flushed at the sharply questioning look he cast her way. "So I read the accident report. I was curious about what had happened."

"If I'd been a better husband, she and our child wouldn't have been killed," he said through clenched teeth. "Nothing can change that fact."

"If she loved you, she wouldn't want you to close yourself off like you have."

"I'm not an easy man to live with. History could repeat itself. I'm not taking that chance."

The thought that had been nagging at the back of her mind and causing her the most hurt refused to remain in the shadows any longer. "The real truth is that you don't love me and you know you never will. Someone else might be able to make you take a chance with your heart, but it isn't me." Her shoulders straight with dignity, she left the room.

Slade watched her go. She was wrong. Loving her would be easy. But he had failed Claudette. He would not risk that kind of failure again.

Chapter Thirteen

Lisa woke the next morning wishing she could take her family and go to a motel, but the evening had ended with a truce on both sides and leaving would only reopen the breach. Saying a silent prayer that Detective Overson would arrest the women today and she could go home, she rose and went into the bathroom.

Her last encounter with Slade played through her mind. It still stung. Splashing cold water on her face, she toweled dry, then stared sternly at herself in the mirror. "You will find someone one day who will love you," she told the image, adding a nod of affirmation to emphasize her words.

Leaving the bathroom, she stuck her head into Andy's room. He wasn't in his bed.

"He's with his father." Morning Hawk's voice sounded from behind her. "They've had breakfast and gone for a ride. Slade wants Andy to become acquainted with the land."

Lisa paled. "Andy's riding his pony out on the range?"

Morning Hawk gave her an indulgent look. "He is with Slade on Slade's horse. My great-grandson will see that no harm comes to the boy." She continued to regard Lisa sagely. "I have listened to the others talking. They all say they want what is best for you, Slade and your child and they agree that what is best is that you and Slade go your separate ways but share in the raising of your child. They're wrong. I have seen the aura that surrounds the three of you when you are together."

"And did you see Claudette there, as well?" Lisa asked caustically. "Because she is always at Slade's side and will always be there."

"Slade needs you. It is not good for him to spend the rest of his life alone."

"Slade doesn't need anyone. And he's not alone. He has his ghost." Without giving Morning Hawk a chance to respond, Lisa strode back into her room and finished dressing. She would not allow this ancient woman to cause her to begin having fantasies about her and Slade as a couple again. Before leaving her room, she spent a few minutes building herself a wall against him.

In the kitchen she found Ester humming while working on the crossword puzzle in the paper. "You're very chipper today," she said, fighting to keep the edge of agitation out of her voice. She knew it wasn't fair to be angry with Ester for being in a good mood, but she was in misery and she thought her aunt should at least show some sympathetic pain.

"I had a talk with White Moon. She explained about Slade's former wife and how he has closed himself off. We both agreed that it was his loss that he wouldn't open his heart to you."

So Ester was happy because the women were all in agreement that she would be a good wife to Slade. Well, even Slade was in agreement on that point. *It's his loss, but I'm the one who's hurting,* she thought grudgingly, then scowled at herself. She would find someone better than him.

Pushing him from her mind, she made herself some breakfast. She had just finished eating when Detective Overson called to inform her that Dorothy was meeting with Claire and Paula later that morning. If she could get them to incriminate themselves, he and his men would move in immediately. He also had search warrants for the women's houses, which his men would serve while the women were with Dorothy. He didn't want them tipped off ahead of time.

Hanging up, Lisa said another prayer that the man would get all the evidence he needed and she could go home and get back to her life.

Too tense to remain inside, she went out onto the front porch, but was too restless to sit. Instead she leaned against one of the pillars supporting the roof and stared out at the vast, open landscape. A sense of aloneness filled her. It was as if a part of her was missing. Slade's image filled her mind. "No," she growled at herself. It was Andy she missed, she insisted, and thinking of her son did cause the aloneness to subside...almost.

Leaving the porch, she rounded the house. A large tree offered shade and a view of the corrals and stables. Wandering over to it, she leaned against the sturdy trunk and scanned the landscape. Realizing she was actually looking for Slade, she told herself she was anxious to see Andy, to make certain he was all right.

And when Slade and Andy did finally come into view

and she experienced a rush of pleasure, she assured herself that it was due entirely to the sight of her son.

Spotting her under the tree, Slade guided his horse toward her.

"Mommy. Meee ri-idee," Andy spouted proudly, sitting up as straight and tall as he could in front of his father.

"I see that," she replied, concentrating only on him and avoiding looking at Slade as much as possible. The fact that Slade had not even attempted to deny the final accusation she'd flung at him last night was a wound that was festering more and more by the second.

Slade lifted Andy off the saddle and lowered him to the ground. Remaining seated in the saddle, his expression shuttered, he said, "You were wrong last night. If I was to ever love another woman, you would be at the top of the list." Then, giving his horse a nudge, he rode away.

Lisa stood staring after him. Had he only said that to trick her into changing her mind and staying? She found it difficult to believe Slade Logan would lie. He was the most honorable man she'd ever known. Hope started to sprout, then Andy tugged at her hand, reminding her of his presence and her cynical side put a quick stop to the new bud. Slade was very attached to his son and might say anything to keep Andy, it argued. "Besides, even if he was being honest, he's also a man with a will of iron and that will of iron is determined to not love me," she reminded herself out loud.

"Mommy?" Andy studied her with a questioning look on his face.

"It's nothing important, sugar," she said, kissing him on the cheek, then guiding him to the house.

But at the door, she paused to look back at Slade. He'd

never looked more ruggedly handsome and her blood heated. "Please, let Detective Overson call soon and tell me it's safe to go home," she pleaded under her breath.

It was early afternoon when her plea was answered. She got a call from the detective saying Claire and Paula had been taken into custody.

Going out onto the porch where Slade was sitting in a rocker, dozing, she woke him. "It's over. My family and I can go home now."

Slade sat for a long moment scowling at the distant landscape. Breaking his silence he said, "We're going to have to work out some kind of visitation schedule for me and Andy."

"That's going to be a little difficult with the distance between us, but you're welcome to come visit whenever you like and he can come here every so often."

"Any chance you'd consider moving back to Lubbock?"

She hated admitting even to herself that it hurt being in his presence, knowing that he preferred a ghost to her. "No."

The grim expression on Slade's face told her he didn't like her decision, but he nodded his acceptance.

"I'm going to make plane reservations for us as soon as possible." Without waiting for a response, she strode back into the house.

Three hours later after she'd signed the papers Slade's lawyer had drawn up, she, her mother, her aunt and Andy boarded a plane for Seattle.

Watching the plane take off, Slade experienced an intense sensation of aloneness. *Better to feel lonely than guilty for causing the death of someone I lo—* He cut that thought off. "I care about Lisa, but I don't love her," he assured himself curtly. The words felt like a lie.

Leaving the airport he drove to the cemetery where Claudette was buried. There the memories of his grief were the strongest and he used them to fortify the wall that kept Lisa out of his heart. The thought that she had already penetrated his defenses taunted him. It was best that she'd left, he told himself.

Several hours later, Lisa paced the living room floor of the house she shared with her mother and her aunt. It was late, very late. Andy and the others were in bed, but she couldn't sleep. She missed Slade.

"Ooh, I hate admitting that," she groaned angrily.

Seeing light from under the door of her mother's room, she knocked lightly, opened the door and found her mother reading. "I can't sleep, either," she said. "I'm going to my office and put things in order."

"Can't that wait until morning?" Helen asked, regarding her daughter worriedly.

"No." Without giving her mother time to protest, Lisa closed the door and left.

At the office, she sorted through her mail, jotted down the phone numbers left on her answering machine by possible new clients and tried to not think about Slade. But his presence lingered. So acute were her memories of him, even with her eyes open she could visualize him there with her.

"Why couldn't he be someone who is easily forgettable?" she mumbled. That answer was easy. If he had been, she'd never have gotten mixed up with him in the first place. Leaning back in her chair, she closed her eyes and his image became so strong, it was almost as if he was in the room with her. Frustration raged through her and she found herself reconsidering the possibility of having a life with him. Then, in the background behind him a faint ghostly image began to appear. She popped her eyes open and cursed under her breath.

Leaving the office, she drove home and went to bed. But even in sleep there was no escape. Slade haunted her dreams.

Late the next morning, as she splashed cold water on her face to try to rid herself of the lingering grogginess of a bad night's rest, the truth suddenly struck her. She was jealous of a ghost. "And there is no reason to be," she snapped at the image in the mirror. It was Slade's guilt and fear that kept him from opening his heart...not Claudette.

In her mind's eye she saw him watching her board the plane. His jaw had been set in a hard line and he had a grim expression of acceptance on his face. The imagery continued and she pictured him alone in his home, letting his guilt eat at him, robbing him of any joy. And she had brought joy into his life. He'd relaxed with her, smiled and laughed. And he'd been tender. Her body trembled at the mere thought of his caress.

A look of purpose spread over her face. Morning Hawk was right. Whether Slade was willing to admit it or not, he needed her. And then there was Andy. He'd formed an instant attachment to Slade. "And he should have a chance to have a full-time father."

A tint of embarrassment at her own weakness turned her cheeks pink as she also conceded that she wanted to be with Slade. No other man could ever have the hold on her heart that he did. "Besides, it would be stupid to give up a good man," she finished.

Marching into the kitchen, she found her mother and

aunt there feeding Andy his midmorning snack. "I'm going back to try to make a go of my marriage to Slade."

Both women looked at her in stunned silence.

It was Helen who found her voice first. "You're going back?"

"If you're doing this for Andy's sake, I don't think that's such a good idea," Ester chimed in.

"I'm doing it for my sake and Slade's. Whether he knows it or not, he needs me. And I need him. He makes me feel complete. I've tried not to, but I love him. And he's always been kind and good to me." A grimace spread over her features. "He also frustrates the heck out of me, but then it's been my observation a great many men are the main source of frustration for the women in their lives."

"True," Ester agreed.

Helen continued to regard her with concern. "Are you really sure this is the right thing to do?"

"My gut instinct tells me that it is."

"Just remember that if things don't work out the way you want them to, you can always come back here," Helen said, rising and giving her daughter a tight hug.

"Absolutely," Ester added, joining in the hug.

It had been five days since Lisa had left. And, each day, instead of being less and less on Slade's mind, she haunted him more. Having Katrina and Boyd around had been a distraction but they'd now moved back into their own place. Left to himself, ever since he'd come home today, he'd been sitting in his favorite chair in the living room, in the dark. His sense of aloneness was so intense it was like a physical pain. Memories of the intimacy he'd shared with Lisa taunted him and he wanted her in his arms.

Then there was Andy. Just a smile from his son made him feel glad. "It's better this way," he said out loud, using the sound of his voice to add substance to his words. The image of Claudette slamming out the front door, followed by the one of her lying on the table in the morgue, burned into his mind like a hot brand.

The sound of a car pulling into his driveway brought a groan of irritation. He was in no mood for company, he thought as he switched on the porch light and stepped out the front door.

For a moment Slade froze at the sight of Lisa's car. He thought maybe he was hallucinating. Or maybe it was someone else and he just thought it looked like her car. Then the driver climbed out and, even in the pale light of the moon, he knew it was her.

Recovering from the shock of seeing her, fear raced through him. Whatever had brought her back had to be serious. Striding down the porch steps, he reached her in moments. "What's happened now?"

"Nothing," she said stiffly.

Slade regarded her skeptically. "Nothing?"

Lisa studied him. His expression was shuttered, giving her no clue as to whether he was glad to see her or not. But then, she'd expected the wall to still be there between them. Her jaw firmed with resolve. This time she would not walk away without a fight. "I've decided that you need me and Andy needs a full-time father."

"You've decided to try to make our marriage work?"

His tone was harsh. If the hand on her arm hadn't tightened so possessively, she'd have been certain he was going to tell her that he'd changed his mind and wanted her to get lost. *I'm making a big mistake,* she thought, panicky. Still, she heard herself saying, "Yes."

Realizing he was still holding on to her, Slade released his grip. *This isn't safe,* his inner voice insisted. But he could not make himself send her away. It was his duty to take care of her and his son, he told himself. "Then we should get you and Andy inside and settled in," he said in a businesslike tone.

"Yes, we should." On the outside, she appeared and sounded like a woman confident in her mission. On the inside, doubts assailed her.

Letting Slade get Andy out of his car seat, she opened the trunk and lifted out one of the lighter suitcases. As they headed toward the house, she realized that the interior of the house was entirely dark. "You forget to pay your electricity bill?"

"I was tired when I got home. I lay down and fell asleep."

She caught the slight hesitation in his voice and noted that he didn't look at her when he spoke. He was lying. He'd been sitting there in the dark, brooding. She'd made the right decision. Whether he was willing to admit it or not, he did need her.

Andy was restless from long days of riding in the car. While Slade carried in the rest of the things she'd brought, she let her son toddle around the guest bedroom across from the master bedroom. This would be Andy's room and she wanted him to get acquainted with it.

Slade carried in the Portacrib. "Guess this will have to do until we can get him a proper bed he won't be able to fall out of," he said. Then leaving Lisa to set it up, he returned to the car for another load.

Setting up the crib, Lisa noticed that Andy seemed totally at ease.

Slade returned with a couple of suitcases and a box of

toys. Setting the box of toys down, he said, "I'm assuming that I should put your things in the master bedroom."

She looked up at him. His expression was shuttered. There was no way of knowing what he was thinking, but the hint of a question in his voice told her he was giving her a chance to state her boundaries. The thought that it might be prudent to remain apart from him for at least a while to see if this really was going to work crossed her mind. She tossed it out. She'd made her decision. "Yes. The blue suitcases are mine."

Slade's expression relaxed and with a nod of approval, he carried the two suitcases she'd indicated across the hall.

She frowned at his departing back. He'd wanted her in his bed but he hadn't been going to push her into it. The barrier he was determined to keep between them was as strong as ever. The urge to change her mind and insist on sleeping in this room with her son swept over her. Again, her jaw firmed with purpose. She wanted to be with him. Maybe that was wanton and perhaps even stupid, but it felt like the right thing to do.

The worry that she was letting lust do her thinking for her taunted her. "So what if I am? If that's all it is, then I'll get it out of my system so I can get on with my life."

"Mommy?"

She looked to her son to find him regarding her worriedly.

She smiled. "Just having a little argument with myself. It's nothing for you to be concerned about," she assured him.

He smiled back and toddled over to the box of toys and began to pull them out.

Lisa glanced toward the suitcases and decided that she was too tired to unpack tonight. Behind her, she heard footfalls. They stopped at the door. Out of the corner of her eye, she saw Slade lean against the jamb in a comfortable, relaxed pose. His presence felt like a warm cozy touch.

"Looks like Andy is settling in just fine," he said.

She heard the pleasure in his voice. "Yes."

Andy cocked his head, making a sort of lopsided inspection of Slade. "Da?"

Pride swelled within Slade. "Yes. Dad," he confirmed, crossing the room and lifting the boy into the air. Then cradling Andy in his arm, his gaze swept the room, coming to rest on Lisa. "Tomorrow you can take my credit card and go purchase any furniture you need to make this room into a nursery."

Lisa nodded her agreement, confessing to herself that she didn't want to send for the furniture in Seattle. Although she kept assuring herself this was where she belonged, the desire to have a safety net lingered.

Slate took note of the fact that she didn't mention sending for more of their things and realized that she wasn't as committed to staying as she claimed. The thought that it might be best if she did leave again crossed his mind. It had a bitter taste. Having her and Andy here brought a warmth to this house it had lacked since Claudette's death. But as for him needing her, he needed no one. However, he would enjoy her company while it lasted. "I have some leftovers Katrina left behind, or I can order take-out or we can go someplace for dinner."

"Andy and I stopped and ate a couple of hours ago." Lisa saw her son yawn widely. "I think it's time I gave him his bath and put him to bed."

Slade hovered in the background, finding towels and doing what he could to help while mentally he found himself looking forward to going to a toy store and spoiling his son with gifts.

A short while later, Lisa sat sipping a cup of tea and watching Slade make himself a roast beef sandwich. To her surprise Andy had laid down in his bed and gone right to sleep, totally at ease in his new surroundings.

She, on the other hand, wasn't. During the course of their affair, she and Slade had spent most of their intimate moments at her place. Here, she'd felt Claudette's presence and had been uncomfortable. *If I'm going to make this work, I have to remember that she's the ghost and I'm a real flesh-and-blood woman and Slade needs me,* she reminded herself curtly.

"I would have come and gotten you...shared in the driving," Slade said, seating himself.

"I wanted to see your reaction when I showed up," she answered honestly. She had told herself to not expect too much from him, but deep down inside she wished for some sign that she really had made the right decision.

Reaching across the table, he took her hand in his. "I have missed you."

She read the friendship on his face. She was also aware that the barrier keeping his feelings from going any deeper was there, as well. "I missed you, too."

Slade relaxed. She was willing to accept their relationship on his terms. His appetite, which had been slack these past days, returned full-force and he ate.

Lisa recognized the signs of a male content in his confidence that he was in control of his world. *Overconfidence comes before a fall,* she told herself encouragingly. "It's been a long day, I'm going to go take a shower and get ready for bed."

Slade caught the small, quirky half smile she tossed

his way and recognized it as an invitation. He wolfed down the rest of his dinner, then headed to the bedroom. The water in the master bath was running. Shedding his clothes, he went in and climbed into the shower with her. "Thought you might like someone to wash your back."

Lisa's body temperature rose at the sight of him. "That would be nice." As he began soaping her, she had to fight to keep herself from purring. His touch was delicious.

Slade had to admit that everything about this moment felt right.

They washed each other, caressing and playfully tickling, then toweled each other dry.

As they left the bathroom and entered the bedroom, Lisa turned her full attention for a moment to the baby monitor and listened.

Slade noticed the sudden loss of her attention and smiled. "I peeked in on Andy before I came in here. He was sleeping peacefully."

Lisa smiled back as he scooped her up in his arms and carried her the rest of the way to the bed.

His caresses and kisses awakened her body to new heights and she could only think about how naturally they fit together when he took possession.

As they moved in the age-old rhythm of union, Slade again found himself thinking that Lisa suited him physically in every way. It was as if their bodies had been made for one another. Then all thought vanished as they reached the summit together and allowed themselves to be lost in the erotic pleasure of the moment.

Chapter Fourteen

Lisa sat on the back porch watching Slade play with Andy. It was a lazy Saturday nearly two months since she and Andy had arrived here. It was clear the bond between the males was steadfastly strong. And she knew Slade cared for her, but she was also aware that he never allowed that caring to go beyond a designated point.

"No marriage is perfect," she murmured out loud. She and Slade truly liked each other. When he came home from a hard day, he talked to her. They communicated about everything...well not everything. She never mentioned Claudette or her frustration that the woman's presence continued to linger in this house. There had been several times when she'd wanted to ask him if they could sell this place, but she knew that moving wouldn't solve the problem. He took Claudette with him wherever he went.

A sense of futility swept through her and she wondered if she could really live with Claudette's ghost for the rest of her life. She'd thought she could. The problem was that she loved Slade with all her heart. Silently she cursed the catch-22 she found herself in. Because she loved him, she couldn't leave him. He needed her to look after him, to see that he ate properly, to be his friend so that he would not be alone. But it was that same love that tormented her because she wanted him to love her back.

"Hey, I need help to escape," Slade called to her, playfully pretending that Andy had him penned down. Immediately, she shoved the disquieting thoughts from her mind and joined them.

All three tumbled around in the grass, laughing and tickling each other. Then Slade suddenly kissed her on the nose and the look in his eyes took her breath away. She knew he was seeing only her and there was love there. Joy raced through her.

The next morning she hummed as she fixed breakfast. She had made the right decision, after all. Smiling contentedly, she went looking for Slade to tell him that his meal was ready.

She found him in his study, standing at his desk with his back to the door. In front of him she could see an ornately carved wooden box. His concentration on its contents was so intense, he didn't even realize she'd entered.

Stopping a couple of paces behind him, she watched as he picked up a photograph and stared at it for a long moment. From where she stood, she could not make out the faces, but the photo was of a couple in wedding garb and she knew without any doubt that it was Slade and Claudette. Reaching back into the box, he picked up a small gold band. Lisa's gaze went to the other contents of the box. It was filled with memorabilia…letters, photos, a couple of pieces of women's jewelry. And she had no doubt they were all reminders of Claudette.

Tears of frustration filled her eyes. He had let down his shield for a moment, but now he was rebuilding it as strongly as ever. She would never win. Quietly, to not let him know she'd observed him, she went to get Andy and took him into the kitchen. The pain she was feeling was more intense than any she'd experienced before.

"I was stupid to come back. I knew this would happen and it will keep happening and each time it will feel worse until I go numb," she told her son, knowing he didn't understand what she was saying, but needing to speak the words out loud. "I know you've grown very attached to your father and I'll see that you get to see him as often as possible, but I can't live my life in the shadow of a ghost."

Andy looked up at her questioningly. "Gho-ost?"

"That's just a figure of speech. Ghosts don't really exist," she assured him. But even as she said this, she found herself thinking that for Slade, Claudette's ghost was as real as the kitchen table in front of her or the chair Andy was sitting in.

Going about the business of seeing that Andy ate, she began to mentally prepare herself for telling Slade she was going back to Seattle. *First and foremost,* she ordered herself, *you will not spill one little tear in front of him.* Having cemented that thought in her mind, she practiced telling him that she didn't feel the marriage was working.

"I don't have time for breakfast this morning." Slade's voice broke into her thoughts. "I've got some errands to run, but I'll be back soon. I'm taking the day off.''

Startled to hear him so close, she turned just in time for him to plant a kiss on her nose. Before she could breathe a word, he'd crossed to Andy, given the boy's hair a tussle, and added, ''You be a good boy for your mother.''

In the next instant he was gone.

Lisa frowned at his departing back. He was a man content with his world while hers lay crumbled in ruins around her.

She was halfway through gathering Andy's things together when Slade returned. ''What's going on?'' he demanded.

''I cannot live in Claudette's shadow,'' she said. ''I thought I could, but I can't.''

''I am no longer haunted by her.''

She straightened to her full height and glared at him. He looked sincere, but she wasn't buying it. ''Don't lie to me, Slade Logan. I saw you in your study with your treasure box of mementos this morning.''

''Mo-ommy. Da-addy.'' Andy looked from one to the other, a stricken expression on his face.

''It's all right, son.'' Slade scooped the boy up into his arms. ''Your mother and I just have a little something to settle. Don't you worry. Everything is going to be just fine.'' Looking to Lisa, he said, ''When you saw me this morning I was saying goodbye. I put the box in a chest in the attic where the rest of Claudette's things are. And one of the errands I just ran was a visit her grave to say farewell. She'll always be a part of my life...a part of my past. But you and Andy are my present, my future.''

Lisa wanted to trust him, but she would not allow herself to be his fool. "I don't believe you. You put the box away because you were afraid I might touch it and taint it. And you're only saying that you've put Claudette behind you because you want Andy to be an everyday part of your life."

"You're wrong." Taking her by the hand, he pulled her along with him and Andy out of the house.

"We're not going anyplace with you," she protested. "We're going back to Seattle."

"I know I've been difficult, stubborn, hardheaded and all the rest. But I love you."

Lisa nearly stumbled over her own feet. She couldn't believe those words had come out of his mouth. She'd never known him to lie, but she still had her doubts. "You love me?"

"I have for a long time. It just took me this long to admit it to myself." They were at his truck now and he was buckling Andy into the safety seat.

Lisa stared at the back of his neck. "Look me in the eye and tell me again."

Finished securing their son, Slade turned to her. "I love you."

The heat in his eyes and the tenderness on his face took her breath away. But the joy that should have flowed through her was blocked by a dam of fear. He looked as if he was telling the truth and he sounded as if he was telling the truth, but she couldn't get the image of him with his box of mementos out of her mind.

"Now, climb in. There's something I need to do."

Too numb to even speak, she did as she was ordered.

Slade drove to Boyd's and Katrina's place. "Katrina is going to watch Andy for us," he said, climbing out and unfastening their son. "Today, he can't go where we're going. I don't want to have to worry about him. This is our time.''

Lisa watched from the truck while he carried Andy up to the door and handed him over to Katrina. Closing her eyes, she envisioned Slade telling her that he loved her. With every fiber of her being, she wanted to believe him. But the fear remained.

''So where are we going?'' she asked when he returned.

''To a place between heaven and earth so that what I have to say to you can be witnessed by both.''

She stared at him. ''That actually sounds romantic, even poetic.''

He grinned. ''Didn't think I had it in me, did you?''

''No,'' she replied honestly.

His grin deepened.

Sitting back, Lisa studied his profile. There was purpose in the set of his jaw. Not knowing what to say, she rode in silence. After a while she realized they were heading in the direction of his mother's ranch.

Entering the property, he didn't stop at the house but continued past it to the open range beyond, finally parking at the base of a mesa. ''This,'' he said when he'd come around the cab and opened her door, ''is my great-grandmother's favorite spot. It is also where I come when I want to do some serious thinking.''

Lisa's gaze took in the untamed land surrounding them. ''It's definitely isolated.''

Taking her by the hand, Slade led her to a narrow ledge that formed a path that wound upward, disappearing around the side of the mesa. Lisa's gaze traveled from it to the summit and she frowned dubiously. ''That's quite a fall if we slip.''

"Trust me."

She met his gaze. "I want to."

"You can."

The sincerity on his face sent a warmth spreading through her. If what he was saying was true, she would gladly follow him through hell and back. Nodding, she allowed him to lead the way.

To her relief, when they reached the part of the path she had not been able to see from below, it cut into the mesa so that they were walled in on both sides, preventing them from falling off the side. Reaching the summit, Slade led her to the middle of the rocky surface.

"This time, I'm doing it right," he said, extracting two rings from his pocket. "This had better fit," he added. "I got the size from one of the rings in your jewelry box and had a friend make these for us."

Lisa could barely breathe as he took her hand in his.

"Pledging my love to you, with this ring I thee wed," he said, slipping it onto her finger.

Lisa stared down at the white and yellow gold band, the two metals worked into an intertwining pattern. The dam holding her joy back burst and tears of happiness began to run down her cheeks.

Slade held the second ring out to her. "I know how difficult I've been. But I'm hoping you feel the same about me as I do about you. If not, I intend to spend the rest of my life trying to win your love."

"You have been more than difficult. But, as hard as I've tried, I've never been able to stop loving you." Taking the ring from him, she slipped it onto his finger. "With all my heart, I pledge myself to you."

Slade laughed with happiness and, scooping her up into his arms, he kissed her. Clinging to him, Lisa began to giggle even while their lips were still pressed together. Never had she felt such happiness or such a sense of oneness with him. Or aloneness...just the two of them together in a world all their own and just as he had promised...someplace between heaven and earth so that both could witness their love.

* * * * *

Beginning in May from

SILHOUETTE Romance

THE TEXAS BROTHERHOOD

A brand-new series by
PATRICIA THAYER

As boys, the ill-fated birthright left to the Randell
brothers by their father almost tore them apart.
As men, they created a legacy of their own....

Don't miss any of their stories!

CHANCE'S JOY (SR #1518)
On sale May 2001

A CHILD FOR CADE (SR #1524)
On sale June 2001

TRAVIS COMES HOME (SR #1530)
On sale July 2001

Available only from Silhouette Romance
at your favorite retail outlet.

Silhouette®
Where love comes alive™

Don't miss the reprisal of
Silhouette Romance's popular miniseries

**When
King Michael of
Edenbourg goes
missing,**

Royally Wed

The Stanbury Crown

**his devoted
family and loyal
subjects make it
their mission to bring
him home safely!**

Their search begins March 2001 and continues through June 2001.

On sale March 2001: **THE EXPECTANT PRINCESS**
by bestselling author **Stella Bagwell** (SR #1504)

On sale April 2001: **THE BLACKSHEEP PRINCE'S BRIDE**
by rising star **Martha Shields** (SR #1510)

On sale May 2001: **CODE NAME: PRINCE**
by popular author **Valerie Parv** (SR #1516)

On sale June 2001: **AN OFFICER AND A PRINCESS**
by award-winning author **Carla Cassidy** (SR #1522)

Available at your favorite retail outlet.

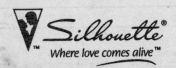

Silhouette®
Where love comes alive™

Visit Silhouette at www.eHarlequin.com

SRRW3